POSTCARDS FROM WAUPACA

Postcards from Waupaca

A collection of short stories

by

A. ELIZABETH HERTING

BOOKS

Adelaide Books
New York / Lisbon
2020

POSTCARDS FROM WAUPACA
A collection of short stories
By A. Elizabeth Herting

Copyright © by A. Elizabeth Herting
Cover design © 2020 Adelaide Books

Published by Adelaide Books, New York / Lisbon
adelaidebooks.org

Editor-in-Chief
Stevan V. Nikolic

For any information, please address Adelaide Books
at info@adelaidebooks.org
or write to:
Adelaide Books
244 Fifth Ave. Suite D27
New York, NY, 10001

ISBN: 978-1-951896-73-7

Printed in the United States of America

This book is dedicated to Aunt Marny and a very special pair of sisters, sitting by a lake, long ago, on a soft summer's evening. My heart lives there with you

The stories in "Postcards From Waupaca" are eclectic, ranging from heart-warming and nostalgic to thought-provoking and speculative. They could easily be enjoyed by a beach on a lazy summer's day, during the holiday season to capture the Christmas spirit or sitting by a roaring fire on that infamous "dark and stormy night." Waupaca is more than just a place, it's a feeling. A destination that lives in the deepest corners of your heart. Come and heed the call of the lake with these memorable and enchanting tales.

Contents

Girl at Mirror

She watched the canoe slicing through the water, the late afternoon sun lighting up the scene like a Norman Rockwell painting. Joannie had just seen her mother's old "Saturday Evening Post" lying on the cabin porch, rushing by it at a dead run on her way to the lake. Rockwell's distinctive imagery imprinted itself onto her imagination as she cannon balled deep into the cool water. The cover pictured a girl gazing at her image in a mirror, a girl who looked to be just about Joannie's age that summer. "Girl at Mirror" was featured in the March 6, 1954 issue of the Post. It was well over a year old now, but still about as current as her mother Viola would ever get. Magazines were considered a luxury to be savored in their household, read and re-read until they literally fell apart. Her mother never threw a single thing away and for once, Joannie was grateful.

She made a note to go back later and find the magazine, completely intrigued by the girl in the picture. The girl's eyes were cautious, questioning as she compared her face to that of the glamorous Jane Russell in a upturned movie magazine perched on her lap. Just what did the girl see as she examined her own reflection? Joannie knew what she saw in her own mirror—an awkward, overweight ten-year-old tomboy with nails bitten down to the quick. She wasn't at all the dreamy, tempestuous creature her eighteen-year-old sister Marilyn had morphed into, kissing her posters of Bobby Darin and Johnny Ray in their shared room, twice every day. Makeup and boys and bobby socks held no sway over Joannie. Certainly not in Waupaca, Wisconsin when the lake was only mere steps away, the long summer days stretching out before her in an endless, glorious line.

She waded out past the shore, waiting for her father to paddle in. He stalled in the middle of the lake and she could see him lying across the seat, his tanned legs trailing in the water as the waves gently rocked the drifting canoe. The smoke from his cigarette lazily wafted by on the afternoon breeze. Lucky Strikes, she smiled to herself, the only kind he ever smoked.

Joannie decided to swim out to him. He'd always told her that she was born part fish and she was determined to prove him right. Ed was her hero. He could swim a whole mile without stopping, she had seen him do it many times. Joannie wanted to do that too, would do anything to make him proud of her.

She bent down in the shallow water, preparing the perfect launch to propel her on her way when she was rudely tackled from behind. Her brother Eddie had gotten the drop on her. Joannie was distracted, hadn't heard him in time. She wouldn't let him get away with it—this was war! They went down in a soggy heap rolling around in the muddy water, wrestling and laughing as Joannie broke away, using his chest as a springboard and giving him a final splash in the face as a farewell. She'd won this particular battle, but she knew that the war was far from over.

"I'll get you Joannie Macaroni! You just wait and see!" Eddie yelled out after her. Joannie knew she'd have to keep a close watch out later in the day. Eddie was not shy about leaving the occasional frog in her bed or using the new bra that Mom had just given her as a makeshift slingshot. She knew that revenge was coming, just not from which direction.

Her father pretended to be asleep, acting genuinely surprised to see her as she swam up to the canoe. He scooped her up and placed her in the seat in front of him, allowing Joannie to paddle as he guided her arms and they slowly headed back into shore. She treasured their summers on the lake together. Ed sometimes had to work three jobs to support them and most of the time, she barely ever saw him. She adored her handsome father with his thick head of dark salt and pepper hair and bright green eyes. He was "Black Irish" he would say with pride and Joannie always knew that he had a soft spot for her. She was the spitting image of his favorite sister Mabel, everyone always said so. Mabel died in childbirth a few years back leaving her father heartbroken. Joannie was glad that he was so delighted at the resemblance, certainly, no one else was awed by her appearance. Her father always told her not to mind, that someday she would grow into her beauty, just like the duckling and the swan.

The sun began its descent when they reached the shore and beached the canoe. Her father put his arm around her as they turned to watch the sunset, the smell of her mother's roast reaching them from the cabin. Her father chuckled lightly, Vi was notorious for cooking meat until it was black as coal. "Well done, but juicy" she called it. She well knew that her mother's practice of charring food was forged during the Great Depression when they had to cook things to death just to make them safe to eat. Joannie made a silent vow that someday, just as soon as she was able, she would order a huge steak. Rare. In a restaurant. Maybe the Girl at Mirror would join her and they would talk about important things like horrid big brothers and moody teen aged sisters. Movie stars, boys, Bobby Darin and what great mysteries would be solved when they finally, magically grew up.

In the meantime, Joannie was simply content to hold her father's hand as they gathered up the courage to face Vi's pot roast together. Marilyn was staying in tonight, Ed caught her kissing a boy behind the concert hall just last evening. He'd snuck around the perimeter of the lake from their cabin to the hall and come up behind them. Boy, was she ever surprised!

Joannie would never admit it, but she was happy that her sister was caught. That meant that the whole family would be together tonight, maybe even have time for a game or two of cards after dinner. The one thing her mother would never pass up was gambling–it was a family tradition. Joannie would definitely be sure to check her chair before sitting down. Eddie was still on the warpath and an ill-placed pine cone was a real possibility.

The music from the concert hall drifted in through the open window as they sat around the table, talking and laughing. Ed swept Vi up as she was clearing the dishes and danced her around the cabin's tiny living room. Joannie decided that she didn't need Girl at Mirror to talk to after all. Everyone she cared about was right here, in a little vacation cabin on a lake in Waupaca, Wisconsin. On a night like this, Joannie could even tolerate her brother. Almost.

An unspoken truce seemed to be in effect as the three of them watched their parents dancing in perfect synchronicity, the years melting away as they twirled around and around in joyful abandon. The mysteries of growing up would just have to wait. Joannie was not ready to step through the looking glass, not quite yet. She was certain that Girl at Mirror would understand.

Her sister tossed and turned restlessly in the bed. The hospice nurse told her that it could be any time now, but she'd held on for the better part of a week. So much longer than they had expected. She was only sixty-nine, eight years younger than herself. It was brutally unfair that this should happen to her baby sister. Marilyn always said that she'd been there on the day Joannie was born and now it would seem, she would also be there on her very last day. She laughed as she remembered their brother Eddie's reaction upon hearing the new baby was a girl had been, "Oh no! Not another one!"

Marilyn held her hand softly and told the well-loved story again, attempting to soothe Joannie's pain as she prepared to take her leave of the world. Her sister was a great beauty with an adventurous spirit, she laughed and loved, always living life to the fullest. Joannie had been widowed for several years, so Marilyn and her sister's only child had been keeping vigil around the clock as her condition worsened. In the quiet moments, as Joannie's daughter left the room, it was just Marilyn at her side. It seemed fitting that the two sisters should be together in these final moments.

As she continued to talk about their childhood together, Marilyn could feel her sister relax, a sense of calm filling the darkened room. She'd just finished reminiscing about summers on the lake long ago when her sister quietly slipped away, Joannie finally joining the Girl at Mirror in a heavenly, peaceful reflection.

Rockwell couldn't have painted it any better.

Originally published in "The Scarlet Leaf Review," October 2017

Grape Eyeballs

The dream was always the same.

Beth could see them at the old kitchen table, Mom to her left and Dad directly across from her. They'd just finished their weekly family dinner, her parents always insisting on that one night to catch up with one another. The teenager that Beth was then would scoff at the idea, roll her eyes and reluctantly join them before running off with her friends. These days she would give absolutely anything to be at that table, their only child once more, free from the obligations of adulthood and grief. Her parents had been gone for years now leaving Beth to navigate her life in a world without them.

They'd both died fairly young, her father especially, in his sixty-third year. He'd had some sort of attack in his sleep, leaving her distraught mother to find him the next morning. Her mother rebuilt her life from the ground up after that, throwing herself fully into being a grandmother to Beth's three kids. She'd take them somewhere almost every weekend, leaving Beth and her husband some much-needed down time.

The kids would come home overfed and excited from their latest adventure, usually involving garage sales, a movie or some sort of shopping spree. She made a special concoction for the kids called "Grape Eyeballs" involving crackers, cream cheese and grapes. The cream cheese worked as a sort of glue so that the grape perched atop the cracker like a giant, green eyeball. Beth's five-year-old son especially loved Grape Eyeballs and was always after her to recreate grandma's famous dish, but she could never do it justice. Her mother would laugh and bring over another big batch of them, an inside joke between her and her grandchildren.

Her mother's unexpected death from a sudden and aggressive brain tumor caused complete shock and devastation to their family. Beth thought they would have so many more years together. They'd made plans, talked endlessly about the kids and taking family trips, but in the end it made no difference.

Life was cruel that way.

In the dream she was at her place at the table once more, her parents talking and laughing while she sat frozen to her spot. Beth knew she was no longer a teenager, was a grown woman with children of her own, but for some reason she was completely transfixed. She sat in silence as they talked about their day, raising a glass of wine together in a toast.

They were both younger than she remembered, vibrant and full of life as the dinner went on. It was a vivid, colorful dream, so real that Beth could swear they were both living again. She could smell the aroma of her dad's garlic pork roast, her stomach grumbling even as she slept. The intelligence behind her mother's blue eyes was striking as she turned her gaze to Beth and asked her about something that happened in school. Her father looked at her with a familiar, crooked smile as he dished out a large spoon of mashed potatoes onto his plate, both of them waiting patiently for her answer.

It was at this point in the dream that Beth usually woke up, late at night, desperate to fall back asleep and continue the heavenly visit. She had so much that she wanted to say, so many things to tell them. Her father was alive when her girls were very young, but never got the chance to meet his grandson.

How proud he'd have been of this boy who looks so much like him!

It always ended the same way, Beth sitting straight up in bed, regret coursing through her like a physical pain. The dream never came back twice in the same night. She was always paralyzed, unable to break the spell and actually speak to her folks before waking up. The dream returned dozens of times and Beth had yet to say a single word to either one of them.

This time, Beth was determined she would finally break free. As they both looked at her expectantly, she could feel the familiar pull, the edges of the dream beginning to crumble in around her. Beth gripped the sides of her chair and dug in, summoning every ounce of strength she could muster. She saw them begin to flicker, turning back into the spirits they'd both become as Beth struggled mightily to keep herself in the moment. She concentrated hard on her mother's face, seeing that her thick, dark hair was just starting to show more salt than pepper, the first traces of laugh lines lightly dancing across her face. Beth heard her dad clearing his throat, a slight sound of impatience that she was taking so long to answer.

"Your mother just asked you a question, Bethie, how did your science test go today?"

Beth began to shake, the effort of holding onto the dream causing her to twitch wildly in uneasy slumber. She opened her mouth to speak, knowing she had only precious seconds left. Taking a deep breath, she saw her parents beginning to dissolve. Beth let out a primal scream, snapping them sharply back into focus.

"Wait!" Beth yelled, slamming her hands down on her childhood kitchen table, making her parents jump in sudden shock.

"This is going to sound crazy, but I have some things I need to tell you."

The dream went on as Beth poured out her grown-up heart to her parents. They would ask a question here and there, occasionally looking across the table at each other in mutual concern. Beth was terrified her chance would slip away, using every possible second she had to tell them about her family and their future grandchildren. Her father was amused as she went on about her growing girls and the many antics of her son, the precocious little boy he would never get to meet.

They seemed to be humoring her, letting her speak so she decided to take a chance. Taking a deep, fortifying breath, Beth told her parents the exact date of their deaths. She spared nothing, laying it all out in excruciating detail. Her mother ignoring all the warning signs of the brain tumor as typical age-related issues, not going to the doctor until it was way too late. Her father dying in his sleep the night before his annual check up. Beth knew it was only a dream, but saying it out loud gave her an immense sense of peace, all the same.

On and on she went, sharing all the milestones of her life that they'd missed, finally ending by telling her parents how much she loved them. Beth could feel tears streaming down her face as her mother reached out to take her hand, preparing to speak. At that moment, Beth shot up in bed, the dream ending in a sudden, gut-churning rush. She reached up and softly touched her face, astonished to find her cheeks were damp.

After all this time, Beth had finally spoken to them. Feeling like a giant weight had been lifted from her soul, she laid back down and fell into a blessed, dreamless sleep.

Beth slept better than she had in ages, sleeping in well past her usual early morning wake-up time. She could hear the kids milling around downstairs, her eldest daughter banging pots and pans in an effort to make breakfast for her younger siblings. Taking a long, luxurious shower, Beth relived every detail of the dream, thrilled that she'd broken the barrier and actually talked to her folks. Maybe this would be the sense of closure she so desperately needed, a new beginning.

As she was getting dressed, Beth heard the chirp of a new message coming in on the cell. She picked it up, scanning the texts on her way downstairs before coming to a dead stop. Beth sat down heavily on the stair, numb with shock and disbelief.

This cannot be real, I am hallucinating.

She read the message again, tears clouding her vision. Beth checked the number a third time, knowing that she could not possibly be receiving messages from it. The phone had been disconnected over three years ago, right after her mother's death.

"Good morning Hon! Dad and I are on our way over with a big batch of Grape Eyeballs for the kids. See you in about ten minutes. LUV"

Beth began to rock back and forth, tightly shutting her eyes before opening them again to see if the message was still there. It was.

Ten minutes? This message came in nearly twenty minutes ago!

The sound of a car door slamming brought her back, footsteps coming up the driveway.

This is not happening, I am still dreaming.

Beth clung to the handrail, carefully making her way down the stairs. Was her dream not really a dream, but something else entirely? She'd heard the old saying, "love conquers all," but was it true? Could love actually conquer death?

I am about to find out, Beth thought as her mother's musical laughter wafted in through the window. Her father said something in reply, his voice rich and sonorous. A voice she had not heard in over ten years, had never expected to hear again.

Not in this life anyway.

Beth composed herself as best she could, feeling euphoria and terror all at the same time, as she walked over to the door and prepared to receive her once-deceased parents.

Originally published in Terror House Magazine, December 2019

The Note

Jack Thornton stood indecisively against the wall, feeling her presence all the way down the long hallway without ever seeing her. He could always sense when she was near, keeping one eye out at all times just in case she should suddenly appear. Jack was not a stalker, would never in a million years think of himself that way. He was just a guy with a serious crush and a serious problem. How would he ever get up the nerve to tell her how he really felt?

She didn't notice him as she passed by, surrounded by her two best friends, deep in some mysterious, feminine conversation. Jack sighed as he caught a whiff of lemon, trying to hang onto the scent as long as he could before it faded away. He couldn't exactly place it–her favorite shampoo, perfume or lotion perhaps? Whatever it was, it immediately made his heart beat a little faster as he went over in his mind, for the millionth time, what he could possibly say to win her over.

Mary-Kate Miller. The name rolled off of his tongue like the sweetest song he'd ever heard as he worked out the perfect turn of phrase to catch her attention. It was a beautiful, traditional name for a one-in-a-million girl. His best friend Taylor kept teasing him, pushing Jack to go and talk to her in the cafeteria at lunch. Every day, Jack would swear that this would be the day that he would finally do it, usually making it a few steps in her direction before turning around in defeat. Normally Jack was a pretty outgoing guy, able to talk to anyone in a social situation, but the feelings that he had for Mary-Kate were turning out to be anything but normal.

There she sat, a vision of loveliness in her pale pink sweater, the center of attention as she always was. Everyone seemed to be drawn to her without even knowing it. She had the bluest eyes he had ever seen, captivating and intelligent. How could he possibly hope to compete with the group of admirers who surrounded her day in and day out? Jack agonized over it for weeks before coming up with the perfect solution. If the spoken words wouldn't come, he would find a different way to pour out his heart. Jack decided to write a note.

Jack sat in his room and thought about the best way to go about it. He instinctively knew that such things should never be texted or emailed, even in this modern age. No, it had to be heartfelt and handwritten, getting his feelings across without sounding desperate or needy. It was an extremely fine line he needed to walk, but he knew that Mary-Kate was well worth the effort.

He'd always been pretty good with words, getting good grades in all of his English classes. Jack was also a voracious reader and enjoyed writing. Maybe he could write something so spectacular that Mary-Kate would instantly become smitten and agree to go out with him. He sat at his desk, the blank page before him and took a deep, cleansing breath.

Nothing. He got up and walked around the room, trying to clear his mind. He tried thinking of all the things he liked about her and decided that if he were to write them all down, the note would soon become a novel. He needed to keep things short and sweet, just enough to give him an opening. He picked up his pen and began:

Dear Mary-Kate,

I know that you don't know me very well, but I have admired you in secret, wanting to tell you how much I

Jack ripped the paper off of his desk and balled it up in frustration. He threw it at the trash can in the corner and watched as it hit the rim and fell to the floor, crushing any lingering dreams of basketball fame. Four, five, then six more balled up notes joined the first as Jack continued his vigil late into the night, writing and rewriting until his hand ached. He tried writing her a poem, but the words sounded too clunky and awkward. He talked about her beauty, her kind heart, and intelligence. He tried giving her clever clues as to his identity but thought that might come off as too childish. Every word, absolutely all of it went into the trash as the hours continued to tick by.

Finally, Jack decided to keep it simple. He folded up the note and wrote her name neatly on the envelope, placing it next to a single pink rose that he'd picked up earlier. He hoped that the little plastic watering tube would keep it fresh until morning. Jack also enclosed a small gift, something he was certain she would like. He'd done his research, quietly observing and talking to her friends, trying to glean as much information as he possibly could and felt confident that his gift would be a hit.

Mary-Kate lived nearby, they were practically neighbors. Jack decided to leave the note at her door then hurry off before she could see him, praying that his plan would work and she would meet with him. Everything finally completed to his satisfaction, he flipped off the light over his bed and settled down to sleep, his stomach a jumble of nerves and anticipation.

Mary-Kate Miller was getting ready, applying her makeup carefully in her lighted mirror when she heard a hurried knock at the door. She sighed and looked at her watch–Maddie was fifteen minutes early as usual. Most of the time, Mary-Kate was only half-dressed when her friend would show up, wanting to gossip with her while she rushed around to finish her morning routine. It looked like today would be no different. She finished her mascara and padded over to the door, getting ready to admonish her friend as she pulled it open to find no one there. Puzzled, she looked down and saw a rose on her doorstep with some kind of note attached to it. She carefully picked it up, looking around to see if anyone was there. She lifted the rose up to her face and breathed in deeply. Pink roses were her absolute favorite. Mary-Kate went back inside and closed the door, lost in her thoughts. *Who would leave her a note?* She really had no idea, she hadn't gone out with anyone since that disastrous spring dance with Peter Vernon. She remembered he had stepped all over her feet, ruining her new white pumps and giving her painful bruises that lasted for well over a month. It couldn't possibly be him.

Mary-Kate slowly opened the note as an object fell from the envelope and into her hand. It was a pendant on a delicate chain, a tiny golden bee. She felt a hot blush rising to her cheeks, noticing that the words on the page were neat and precise.

Dearest Mary-Kate,

Would you bee-lieve?
Please make me the happiest guy in the entire world and agree to have an early dinner with me this afternoon, 4:00 in the cafeteria.

Yours Truly,
An Admirer

Mary-Kate loved bees. Her room was decorated with them, she had bee pins, earrings, and scarves. She adored the little creatures, was enchanted that her secret admirer had known this and would give her such a thoughtful gift. *Who could this possibly be?* She wracked her brain, going over every possibility: who it might be, who she really wanted it to be. A loud knock on her door shattered her romantic musings. Maddie must be here at last. Mary-Kate went over to let her in, thinking of just the perfect outfit she would wear along with her new bee pendant when she went to meet her secret admirer later in the day.

Jack went through his daily routine in anguish, watching the minutes on the clock slowly tick by. He'd arranged everything for their first meeting with great care. Denny, the cafeteria manager was an old friend of his and owed him a favor or two. He'd agreed to let Jack have the cafeteria at four o'clock before opening the doors at five for their regular dinner service, giving them a full hour for a private, and hopefully romantic, dinner. Jack and his buddy Ralph Taylor went in to decorate the place, hanging Chinese lanterns from the ceiling and setting the best corner table with a crisp white cloth and the finest silver cutlery. He brought down two crystal goblets from his place and opened up a bottle of dry red wine, letting it breathe. To top it all off, he lit two taper candles and asked Denny to play his favorite Sinatra album softly on the overhead speakers. It was spaghetti night, his favorite night of the week. Jack fervently hoped that Mary-Kate would be there at the appointed time and would agree to have dinner with him.

Taylor punched him on the arm, wishing him luck and hightailing it out of the cafeteria just before the clock struck four. Jack stood and smoothed down his best blazer, the one with the tan suede on the elbows and adjusted his tie. He'd polished his shoes just this morning after rushing back into his apartment, out of breath after leaving her the note. She lived four doors down from him and had said good morning every day for the past year, never knowing the profound effect she was having. God! How he hoped she would agree to go out with him.

Sinatra's sultry voice began to croon his favorite song, "The Second Time Around" as he stood, ramrod straight, just like in his military days and anxiously awaited her arrival. The door to the cafeteria slowly opened and Mary-Kate Miller walked in, right on time. He was instantly enveloped in the familiar scent of lemon verbena as she came towards him like a dream. He took a big, fortifying breath knowing that he was in deep, deep trouble. The years melted away, and he realized with a sudden shock that he hadn't felt this way since the first time he'd met his late wife, some sixty-odd years before. He'd been widowed for almost ten years now, knew that she'd also lost her husband some time ago. Was there any chance that she might ever consider him? Well, he thought nervously, he was about to find out.

She wore a lovely floral pattern dress, the bee pendant he'd given her prominently displayed around her elegant neck. She styled her long, flowing white hair down around her shoulders like a girl and Jack marveled that he couldn't even guess her age, so youthful and beautiful did she appear in that moment. He swallowed hard as she approached him and he offered her a second long-stemmed pink rose. His carefully prepared speech went right out the window as he looked into her deep blue eyes and found real affection there, giving him courage.

"Hello Mary-Kate. Would you bee-lieve?"

She reached out to him, taking his hand in hers and saying softly, "I would, Jack Thornton, for I've had my eye on you for quite some time now. I thought you'd never ask."

Without saying a word, he took her gently into his arms as they began to sway in time to Sinatra, the words etching themselves onto his heart.

"Who can say what brought us to this miracle we've found?
There are those who'll bet love comes but once, and yet
I'm oh, so glad we met the second time around"

They continued to dance around the cafeteria, completely oblivious to the outside world under the soft glow of the paper lanterns. Taylor and a few of the residents peeked in through the windows, watching them move together, already matched in perfect sync. Denny and the kitchen crew crept quietly back into the kitchen, not wanting to interrupt their dance. The plates of spaghetti went back into the oven, for love was in the air at the Happy Haven Retirement Community and dinner could wait.

Ralph Taylor turned and smiled at Maddie Travis, holding out his hand for a spontaneous dance right there in the lobby, following his best friend's example. Maddie giggled a little, taking his hand and twirling around him like a giddy schoolgirl. They both understood in that moment, one universal truth that any of the residents in the Haven would happily agree with: that when it comes to love, there is no time like the present and age is nothing but a number.

Originally published in "Edify Fiction," May 2017

Guardian Angel
of the Commissary

Two toddlers.

Tami felt an intense flash of deja vu as her younger son grabbed a fistful of peanut M&Ms from the display next to the check out line and attempted to shove the entire bag, unopened, into his mouth. She quickly decided that whomever was in charge of designing grocery stores couldn't possibly be a mother. If there was any place in the world that gave hell a run for its money in the torture department, it was the candy and gum display at the Commissary with two small toddlers in tow.

The deja vu feeling was making her dizzy, so strong was the memory from just one year ago. Back then, she'd had only one toddler with a bun in the oven and a missing-in-action husband, one booted foot firmly planted out the door.

They'd married impossibly young, Tami sneaking away from her parents home in the middle of the night and throwing herself into his eager arms.

Milo was Army, scooping her up and depositing her onto the base into a perfectly adequate row house that looked like all of the others on their pseudo-block. It was pure infatuation, true love unlike anything she'd ever known before. It was heaven right up until it was hell, Tami being just eighteen years old when they wed in a furtive ceremony at the county courthouse.

She'd found over the past couple of years that while old high-school friends were just beginning to graduate from college like maturing blooms in a garden, Tami was growing her own hothouse flowers. She'd bet it all on Milo and lost, the fires of youthful passion burning themselves out in a pathetic whimper.

It was particularly galling that while Milo was in the process of moving out, Tami gave birth to their second son. The baby was the spitting image of Milo, indistinguishable from his old baby pictures, fate's way of getting the last laugh.

She may not have her husband anymore, but she would raise his doppelganger right along with his older brother, Liam, who had just celebrated his third birthday.

She closed her eyes and tried to tamp down the familiar feelings of dread as she pried the candy away from Zachary's needy fingers. Tami turned to the older lady behind her with the apologetic mea culpa of a frazzled young mother, placing her hands protectively over her swelling belly.

Tami's latest hothouse flower had been from a second hasty marriage, another military man who promised her the moon and left her behind in the rubble. This latest betrayal was still raw and angry. She'd been so certain that she would never stand in the Commissary again, lost and alone, pregnant and trailing a toddler.

No, this time she was pregnant. And alone. With two toddlers.

Tami would laugh if she didn't think it would set her off on a tearful jag in front of God and everyone, right there in the checkout line. She swallowed hard and gently moved Zachary out in front of her and away from the candy, ignoring the blatant stares from disapproving shoppers. The worst part would be when she broke out the food stamps. The unspoken judgment, hanging heavily in the air, always cut her to the quick.

In another life she'd be going to parties, perhaps shopping for the perfect dress with girlfriends or well on her way to getting a degree. Instead, here she stood, knee deep in shameful recrimination, trying desperately to disappear into the tabloid magazine racks.

Tami had just celebrated her twenty-first birthday.

Could this line possibly take any longer?

Master Sergeant Otis T. Hudson was not in the habit of waiting. Efficiency was his stock in trade, the young recruits that flowed through the base like so much greenhorn infested water only had so much time before they needed to become real, fighting men. Invincible men in this old man's Army.

Check that, Hudson, you ancient, crusty old fart. Men AND women. This old man's Army is no longer just a boy's club.

Otis had rankled under the political correctness of this latest directive at first, until he had the pleasure of training two of the meanest, nail-spitting women recruits he'd ever seen, both of them putting his toughest men to shame. He was a believer after that. It was a rarity, but entirely possible.

Besides, he had watched his wife Eliza go through labor for thirty-six hours with his daughter, watching in sheer terror until he was sure he would pass out before she presented him with their precious girl, Elizabeth.

Eliza was cool and confident with their newly-minted daughter in her arms, like they were going to a Sunday picnic.

After that, Otis was always of the mind that women possessed a different, deeper kind of strength. It actually scared him a little.

As a black man making his way up the ranks, Hudson didn't have time for excuses or bullshit. He'd scratched and clawed his way up, choosing to do it the hard way, having to work that much harder to prove his merits past any affirmative action or quietly held racism.

Otis would earn it in his own way or not at all. He saw no earthly reason why the female recruits could not do the same, thus changing a firmly held belief in his mind. Actions to him spoke way louder than words.

His wife always said he was as stubborn as a mule with a golden heart. Otis didn't know about that, but as he approached his final, retirement year he found his patience sorely lacking.

Especially when he had only five items in his cart and he'd been standing here for over fifteen minutes as the older lady in front of him continued to sigh in a fake, over-dramatic fashion.

"Excuse me, do you know that your little boy has put that candy into his mouth? There is no way that should go back on the shelf! It is a health hazard!"

"Ma'am, I am so sorry. He doesn't know any better…"

"Well, he sure could use a dose of good manners! That is sorely lacking in this day and age, why just look at you!"

Tami sunk back, gathering her boys to her side. The random beeps of the scanner causing a fresh batch of panic to break out over her brow. She was raised better than this, deserved better than she was about to get.

Liam screamed, completely unscripted at that moment while Zachary stuck his hands in the candy display once again, flinging packages to and fro. Tami began to do damage control, desperately grasping at the discarded candy bags while her tormentor continued.

"Seriously, you should be ashamed of yourself. A pathetic broodmare sucking off of the public teat. If you had any shame at all, you would just disappear!"

Hot, shameful tears ran down Tami's face. She may not be much in this life, but she was a human being. No one would put her down this way in front of her sons. She took a deep fortifying breath and turned to face the lady.

"Excuse me ma'am, this old Army man would like clarification on something."

His voice was deep and sonorous, the timbre of it causing entire generations of recruits to shake in their brand new boots. Tami saw him standing just behind the angry lady, ramrod straight with his arms at his side in true military fashion.

"Madam, I and all of our fellow travelers in this line would like to be enlightened by you. Can you please tell us, did your parents actually have any children that lived?"

The woman's face turned red as a beet. She stared back at him, incredulous, spitting mad in a fit of imperious glory.

"Excuse me, sir? How dare you speak to me that way!"

"Madam, I most certainly do dare. You will not speak to a woman raising the children of an Army man in such an insulting fashion. In fact, you will speak to her with a civil tongue in your head or you will not speak at all!"

The shoppers all around them burst out in spontaneous applause as the old woman extricated herself from the line in a righteous huff. Tami felt weak in the knees as the older Army man approached her, his voice softening as he shepherded Zachary back towards his frazzled mother.

Otis noticed that she had a smattering of freckles across her nose, just like his Lizzie. The boys looked up at him in astonishment. They were fine boys, Otis could envision them at about eighteen or so, standing in front of him in a long line of fresh recruits. This was a young mother who needed a helping hand, such disrespectful behavior towards her would not happen again. Not if he could help it.

"Thank you, ma'am, for bringing up the next generation. If I could, would you allow me to assist you today?"

Hudson handed the checker his credit card and loaded her bags into her cart, his own five items completely forgotten in the process. He walked her out to the parking lot, speaking in soft tones as she told him about her life and boys until he found himself inviting them all over to the house for dinner later that night. He had a feeling Eliza would approve, she was the one with a heart of gold, not Otis.

Neither one of them could know it at the time, but their encounter in the Commissary would grow into a life-long friendship. He and Eliza would become an integral part of their existence from that day forward, throughout many years. They would even be there with Tami as she was delivered of her third son, an adorable little guy with freckles on his nose that Tami named Otis.

Master Sergeant Otis T. Hudson became the central father figure in the lives of her boys, seeing Liam off to boot camp when he reached his eighteenth birthday, a rash of proud tears running down his kindly old face.

Tami was crying with relief as she pulled away that day, incredibly grateful to her Guardian Angel of the Commissary.

The boys each gave him a sideways salute as he helped them into the car and Otis found himself thinking that maybe he wouldn't retire after all. Eliza would probably want to kill him, but she would understand. Eventually.

An old Army man's work was never done.

Originally published in "Down in the Dirt Magazine," August 2019

The Sentinel

The Sentinel arrives at his post, arranging himself in a way that gives him the very best vantage point. He settles in and can see the entire perimeter unfold before him, from the farthest hill to the closest tree. He readjusts his stance once more, until he is completely satisfied that not an inch of his area is out of view. He stays watchful and silent, always vigilant, always ready at a moment's notice. His is a very important post.

He can hear them before he sees them as they make their way out of the building and spill out onto the grassy field, running and laughing in their mad dash to get into the sun. It is a crisp autumn day, the Sentinel's favorite time of year, and he revels right along with them at the feel of the warm afternoon sun shining down upon his face. He cocks his head to the side— *was that a real scream or one of play?* He decides on the latter and refocuses his energy on a large group running halfway down the main hill of his perimeter. A flying ball catches his attention as it soars high up into the sky, landing in eager, outstretched arms. They all run past him, completely unaware of his presence which is, of course, as it should be. It is a scene of pandemonium as they fan out in all directions, small groups breaking off and reforming into the collective.

The Sentinel closely watches the stragglers, the ones that wander to the outskirts before being shooed back into place by the guard on duty. He hears more yelling, laughing, singing coming at him from every direction, but the Sentinel stands firm. They continue to run, jump, frolic and dance around him like a carnival of brightly colored lunatics, assaulting every one of his senses. Still he remains, unflinching, ever wary and alert.

His is a very important post.

He catches a distinct odor of burning logs on a passing breeze along with a new, urgent smell that instantly raises his hackles, his body taut with alarm. Turning to his right, he sees one of the group chasing what appears to be a brightly colored butterfly down the very farthest hill, almost to the end of his perimeter.

Just out of his line of sight, the intruder lurks, the malice of his intentions hitting the Sentinel in sickening waves. The intruder is nervous, determined as the innocent one blindly wanders into the danger zone. He sizes up the stranger, sees him hold something out to the straggler, talking in brightly soothing tones that the Sentinel immediately knows to be a ruse. A beat up old car with an open door waits on the street, just mere steps behind them. The intruder opens his arms, beckoning and enticing as the innocent one slowly moves forward, unsure, but cautiously trusting. Too trusting.

Every part of the Sentinel is coiled, ready to spring as he watches the awful scene play out in real time before him. The intruder almost has his prize within reach as precious seconds tick by, the two moving closer and closer to each other in a horrific, tragic dance. A dance of disaster. Instantly the Sentinel begins his rescue maneuver, leaping out from his post and bearing down upon the target with deadly efficiency. Every fiber of his being is engaged as he attempts to extricate the innocent while taking out the interloper in a series of swift, decisive blows.

The intruder bellows in fear, alerting the main group and guard as the Sentinel continues his frontal assault with practiced skill. The target is down in a defensive crouch, trying to take cover but it is no use. The Sentinel lets out a primal scream as the guard rushes over, relieving him of his prisoner and whisking the innocent away to safety. Satisfied that both the scene and the intruder are secured, the Sentinel returns to his duty, making sure that the rest of the group are all present and accounted for. With the satisfaction that only comes with a job well done, he resumes his vigil. After all, he is needed and extremely valuable here.

His is a very important post.

Colleen Chase shields her eyes from the bright afternoon sun and watches as her little charges run onto the playground with joyful abandon. It's "Fun Friday" at West Valley Elementary School and this is her last class of the day. As she watches them at play, she feels a sudden burst of joy that she gets to do this every single day, having done so for over five years now.

The field is large, the kids spreading out all over as Colleen makes a mental check of each one, counting and recounting as best she can in the ensuing chaos. Colleen frowns in concentration. *Where did Caleb get off to?* Trying to keep Caleb in one place was like nailing down a puddle of water, but she could usually track him to his favorite spots. She scans the playground equipment, by way of the swings, then looks out to the field where a group of boys are playing a pickup football game. Not finding him in any of those places, Colleen grabs her walkie-talkie and calls in to ask the front office if Caleb left to go home early, which of course she knew, he hadn't.

She decides to head to the bottom of the hill, hoping he has moved temporarily out of view and will still be playing there. Caleb has a tendency to get easily distracted, even more than most first graders do, and she's always careful to keep him in sight. She looks down the length of the hill and is about to turn back, when a movement catches the corner of her eye. Her heart skipping a beat, she sees a strange man holding out a candy bar, Caleb slowly making his way over to him. *This is definitely not a parent,* she thinks, her hand instinctively reaching for the walkie-talkie at her hip. The stranger radiates evil desperation and Colleen knows with a sickening dread that if Caleb gets to the man, it will already be too late. They will never see him again.

She calls in a Code Red and begins to run at full speed down the hill, waving her arms and yelling at Caleb to run away when an incredible sight stops her dead in her tracks. A large crow, possibly the biggest one she has ever seen, swoops down from a pine tree on the outskirts of the playground. Seemingly out of nowhere, it makes a beeline straight for the man, gouging and pecking at him in pure, unadulterated fury. Blood spurts from the man's eye as he desperately tries to ward off his attacker, the crow regrouping and coming at him again and again like a scene from Hitchcock's "The Birds" movie.

The crow screams at the man, a screeching, hellish sound that jolts Colleen out of her temporary shock and back into action. Reaching Caleb, she scoops him up in a protective hug just as the crow has the man down, hands covering his head in abject terror. The first police sirens race down the street and into the parking lot before the crow, with one last defiant caw, reluctantly flies back to his perch in the tallest tree. Colleen watches in weak-kneed relief as the man is led away in handcuffs, Caleb safe and in the arms of his visibly shaken parents. An unspeakable tragedy has been averted here today, with an outcome that Colleen knows could have been very, very different.

The next day, Colleen walks to the tree where she's convinced the crow had perched. She tried to explain exactly what happened to the police, but they were reluctant to believe her—her story is just too outlandish. She was the only actual witness to the events of that day and she begins to think that maybe it didn't happen after all, it was all in her mind. Finding the tree, she shields her eyes, looking far up into the distant branches. Colleen isn't expecting to find anything, actually feels kind of stupid when all of a sudden, she sees him there up on the highest branch. He is a fine looking specimen as far as crows go. Big and proud and black as ink, his intense, intelligent gaze looks her over, sizing her up.

A sudden memory fills her mind, something her mother had told her about crows. Mom always said that whenever you look a crow in the eye, you should always salute, every single time. That never made any sense to her when she was a kid, but she definitely understands it now.

Backing up a few paces from the tree, Colleen makes sure she has the crow completely in sight. With great ceremony, she lifts her hand to her forehead attempting to salute in the crisp, proper way her father taught her. She and the Sentinel lock eyes as she slowly lowers her arm, both taking the measure of the other in mutual wariness and respect. She turns away, feeling immense gratitude that he is there right along with her. Keeping watch, keeping them safe.

Theirs has always been and will always be, a very important post.

Originally published in "Fictive Dream," March 2017

Butterfly Girl

The butterfly floated lighter than air, skimming just above the easy flow and current of the water. The lake was calm with just the slightest hint of a breeze, lifting the delicate little creature high, then bringing it low in a delightful summer's dance. It weaved and bobbed, its bright orange wings catching the noonday sun as a single plaintive loon cried off in the distance.

The lake was teeming with life, seen and unseen. Countless numbers of fish traversed its waters, a symphony of life and death in a million permutations, nature's battles constantly raging. Still, the water remained outwardly calm; a sheet of glass on a torrid July day, an aquatic universe as vast and primordial as the heavens above. The butterfly was unconcerned with any of this, its only function at that moment was simply to be.

The girl sat, still as a statue at the lake's edge, her pole dangling lazily in the water. With all of the urgency of a hot summer day, she laid back onto the dock, lacing her hands underneath her head and gazed up into the clear blue sky. She allowed her mind to drift, all of the matters troubling her thirteen-year-old mind fading away as she felt the sun's glow through her closed eyelids. The girl could have been from any era, her cutoff jeans and castoff sneakers leaving the only trace of time in her otherwise carefree existence. A slight tug at her pole made her pause before drifting back into her pleasant daydream. She had been fishing long enough to know the difference between an honest bite and the gentle pull of the lake.

The butterfly was carried high up into the sky on a burst of air before dropping back to the earth in a gusty spin and landing gracefully onto the dreaming girl's chest. She opened one eye and held her breath, not daring to move and risk dislodging the tiny creature. It extended its wings in supplication, allowing the girl to slowly reach out and cup its resting form in her eager hand.

She lifted her hand to her face with wonder, both the butterfly and the girl regarding each other in silent awe. She could see shades of liquid gold streaming through its paper-thin wings in the afternoon sun, nature's version of stained glass lighting up the cathedral that both girl and butterfly called home. It was a sort of religious experience for the girl who had grown up with skinned knees and sunshine, skimming rocks along the lake's surface just a little bit further with every passing year.

She was on the very brink of womanhood, attempting to hold it back as long as she possibly could, just as she now held the errant butterfly in the palm of her hand. The girl was very aware that these sensations were fleeting. The butterfly and her childhood would carelessly flit away whenever the whim took them, gone forever in an instant. For now, at least, a truce had been called as the girl and butterfly were simply content to bask in the sun together. Beauty was drawn to beauty, as the lake swelled with abundance and the world continued to turn on its axis in complete indifference.

The heat of the day could have caused a mirage for any passing bystander to observe if they truly wanted to see. A gangly, freckled-faced girl holding a butterfly transformed instantly into a stunning lady, hair piled high with dark smoky eyes and red lipstick tracing her pillowy lips. The butterfly twitched its wings and she became a young mother, basking in the joy of her first child as she showed him the proper way to bait a hook. As the sun traveled farther across the sky, a handsome woman of middle years dangled her feet in the water as her growing children splashed and frolicked all around her. Sunset found a grandmother with salt and pepper hair holding a small girl on her knee, pulling a fish from the water as the child squealed in pure, unadulterated delight. The moon had barely begun to rise before the scene of a white-haired lady in a wheelchair appeared in the shimmering dusk. A long-legged girl of thirteen helped her to cast her line far out into the water, the girl's hand gently resting on the old woman's back as the butterfly floated and danced euphorically all around them.

The girl opened her eyes, the vision disintegrating around her as the butterfly raised it legs and prepared to fly. She felt a twinge of melancholy, an emotion she did not yet know how to put into words, as the butterfly lifted off of her hand and took flight. Reluctantly, she gathered up her pole, watching the butterfly once more as it ascended into the clear evening sky before turning back for home.

The girl walked away as the sun finally melted into the lake, another day at an end. The butterfly was unconcerned with any of this. Its only function was simply to be as the lake brimmed with life and the earth continued to turn on its axis in complete indifference.

Originally Published in "Clumsy Quips," October 2017

Unencumbered

Unencumbered.

That really was the perfect word. Dusty Barrett couldn't remember where or when he'd heard it before, only that it had to be the very best word to describe it. That certainty of knowledge spooked him a little, he'd felt twinges of strange in the Slipper before but never anything quite like this.

The balloon bobbed and weaved high above in the rafters, casting shadows on the well worn dance floor below. The polish of the floor shined in the moonlight, giving the balloon an even more surreal appearance as it danced through the air. Dusty found himself leaning on his battered old mop, staring transfixed as it dipped lower and lower on an invisible current before popping back up to its rightful place on the ceiling.

It hovered, tantalizingly out of reach, mocking him in its careless frolic. He racked his brain, trying to recall the first time he had seen it. One event around here always blended into the next and into the next, and so on and so forth, ad nauseum, amen.

There was no shortage of happily-ever-afters in the Crystal Slipper Wedding Emporium, *"the place where dreams are made to fit,"* and certainly no lack of balloons. There were two things, however, that made this straggler stand out from its helium-infused brethren. One was the fact that this particular balloon appeared to be quite a hearty survivor, still flying high long after the lesser specimens had deflated, and the second was in its color.

The balloon was enormous, full to bursting and black as ink. So much so that Dusty couldn't find any trace of light shining through it, the oblivion of a dark winter's night. It gave him the willies, like someone stepping upon his future grave. *Is it a new trend to have giant black balloons at a wedding reception, especially ones like this? Aside from the pierced and tatted-up couples that came in every now and then, he couldn't recall seeing any. Was this balloon really the "must have" staple of the modern bride?*

The balloon made a sudden lunge towards him and Dusty jumped back in shock, dropping his mop with a loud bang that ping ponged across the empty walls. He guessed there must be a window open somewhere in the facility, something to cause it to bob around like that.

Dusty knew his boss wouldn't like it if he left a window open at the end of his shift. He'd been working here for over thirty years, but he didn't dare test her patience. Mai Tran, the latest owner of the Slipper, was a formidable young woman, a no-nonsense daughter of Vietnamese immigrants. She already distrusted him a little, his service in the military hanging between them like an invisible barrier. Dusty served two tours in 'Nam and had no desire to discover if he'd ever faced her grandfather over a rice paddy, so the elephant in the room remained firmly tucked away.

He was rooting for her success. Out of all the owners of the Crystal Slipper, she was by far the best. Hardworking, driven. Dusty recognized these same qualities in himself from long ago. She would have no qualms about correcting him if she could see him standing there, slack-jawed, staring at a balloon instead of finishing his nightly duties. He wouldn't blame her, not a bit. He had plans to retire in the next few years with his reputation intact. Dusty had no desire to lose his job at this late date.

No, it would be better to do his rounds and lock up for the night. The balloon would probably be on the floor by morning and he could throw it away, no harm no foul. He turned back one last time and saw the balloon slowly rising back to the rafters. Quickly turning off the main light switch, he double-timed it back to the lobby with goose flesh breaking out up and down his tired old spine.

Pop-pop-pop!

The rapid-fire rained down around his head as he dove down ass-deep into the muck. He knew the grenades were ever-present, they had just swept the perimeter but there was always the chance that one would be missed. It was fifty-fifty that he would go home or find his grave amongst the mud and mosquitoes and blood of his fallen brothers.

It was then that he saw him. The new recruit screamed in fear and confusion, rising from the ground in a blind panic. Dusty could feel everything slowing down to a snail's pace as he jumped up and began to run toward the terrified young man. They went over like a ton of bricks as two bullets bit angrily into Dusty's back. Luckily he survived his wounds, having saved the recruit in the process.

They sent him home after he healed, giving him a Purple Heart. Dusty placed it in the hand of a grizzled old homeless vet on the street as he passed by. No more would he be beholden to anyone but himself. From that moment on, Dusty would be free.

He would be unencumbered.
POP!

The sound went off like a gunshot, ringing in his ears. Dusty hit the deck, crawling across the dingy old carpet under an invisible tripwire. He could feel the familiar pull of the jungle assaulting his face, the stings of fear and bugs and prickly heat tormenting him as he made his way inch by inch back to the main ballroom. The smell of sulfur and sweat filled the air as Dusty regressed into the posture of a young soldier, the bullets whizzing savagely right above his head. This time he wouldn't be so lucky, he was way too old to survive such a deadly barrage.

An explosion rocked the ballroom just as Dusty pushed open the swinging doors and leaped through. He landed on the slick dance floor, sliding halfway across on his belly in an undignified fashion. The lights were flickering, smoke billowing up all around him. Rapid gunfire, detonated landmines and the whir of a chopper filled his shattered senses until he thought he would explode. There must be something seriously wrong with his mind for, surely, none of this could possibly be real. A final fusillade of impossible sounds attacked him from every direction as he flipped over onto all fours and covered his head, waiting for death to claim him.

In an instant the room went completely silent, causing Dusty to jump up in fright. The sudden absence of sound was worse than the noise. He could still hear the hellish zing of bullets ricocheting around in his brain, but what was even worse than that was the balloon.

It descended slowly, bewitchingly towards Dusty, inflating bigger and bigger as it fell toward him in a deliberate arc. As it got closer, he began to see that it really wasn't just black after all. There were swirling patterns and constellations dancing across its dark surface.

When it became half the size of the main ballroom, Dusty reached out, mesmerized, as he saw within it his mother's hands. She was holding her knitting needles as Dusty sat at her feet, a scene he remembered from long, long ago. Deeper still were flashes of color, sunshine-filled days and fireflies on a humid summer's night; a girl with soulful brown eyes that made his heart flutter; a vision of his buddy Rex bleeding out onto the jungle floor before he died; skinned knees and the perfect jump shot; a kind girl in a Vietnamese brothel, who taught him how to whistle.

The balloon took on the shape of the entire room as it reached Dusty at last, mere inches from his face. Silent tears streamed down the old man's cheeks as he tentatively reached up and touched it with both hands. A warm, euphoric sensation enveloped his body, causing him to laugh in sudden surprise. A liquid golden light, brighter than anything Dusty had ever known, filled his vision as the balloon popped, the immense, gargantuan sound of it blotting out all thought before the bottom fell out of the earth.

Mai Tran wiped away a smattering of tears, angry at herself for crying in public. She was taught to keep emotions private, never to show any sign of weakness, but she could perhaps be forgiven on this particular occasion.

The urn sat on a tasteful platform in the main ballroom, what they used at the Slipper to showcase wedding cakes. Mai would never divulge the platform's current purpose to any future brides however, it would be very bad for business.

Dusty had no family to speak of, he'd never married as far as she knew. It made her impossibly sad to think that she was the closest thing to a friend he'd had in this world. She found him on the ballroom floor, dead of an apparent heart attack. It was only fitting that his service should be at the Slipper after so many years of faithful service.

Only a few people filled the folding chairs as the priest gave Dusty his final blessing; a couple of drinking buddies from the local Legion Hall, some employees from the Slipper and Mai herself. It made her tears fall even faster knowing that they'd found a copy of his will in his rundown apartment, addressed to her. It asked for all of his possessions to be left to the local homeless shelter and he wished to be cremated. If she would, he asked Mai Tran to take his ashes and spread them in Vietnam when she went back for a visit. Dusty would rest where he'd lived the most.

Regret coursed through her at the thought that she'd never let him know how much she actually liked him. She was not overly familiar with the employees, but Dusty was a kind man and a good worker. She would fulfill his final wish, it was the very least she could do. As the few meager souls made their way out of the service, Mai Tran picked up the urn, carefully cradling it in her arms. She would bring Dusty home with her for now, until the trip could be arranged.

Everything had been put away, chairs stacked and the ballroom put back exactly the way it was before. No one here would ever share the details of Dusty's sad fate. The Crystal Slipper Wedding Emporium was a happy place after all, a place where dreams were made to fit. Mai Tran planned to keep it that way.

As she turned to survey the ballroom one last time and turn out the lights, a sudden movement caught her eye. A large black balloon floated way up in the rafters. Mai frowned. *Did someone bring that to the service today? Why on earth would anyone do such a thing?* It seemed completely morbid. The balloon dipped towards Mai on an invisible breeze, unencumbered by gravity, almost taunting her in her somber mood.

Mai Tran sighed and decided to leave it. The balloon's color gave her a feeling of foreboding and she wasn't in the mood for any more darkness tonight. She turned and watched as the balloon floated back up to the ceiling, before turning off the lights and bringing Dusty home.

Originally Published in "Terror House Magazine," December 2018

A South Side Romance

Bob sat on her couch, his head spinning in inebriated anticipation.

It was a whirlwind of a date. Dinner, drinks, and dancing until Jerry Toulouse, the bartender at the Chez Si Bon Lounge, had literally shown them out, firmly locking the door behind them.

Joan was an absolute vision in an emerald green silk dress, accentuating every curve as she danced with him to the romantic strains of "Hang on Sloopy." He'd had to fight off more than one guy tonight, the men gathering around her on the dance floor like moths to a flame. Not that he could blame them. He was the lucky son-of-a-bitch that was there with her, after all.

Bob was well known at the Chez. Toulouse often took his calls behind the bar, usually a young lady trying to track him down. The master of all he surveyed, his world was completely shaken when he saw her walk in that first night. Her dark hair was piled high atop her head, long and luscious, as she took her seat with a friend. Barflies like Louie "The Lip" and Tommy Espinoza circled their table like lions on the hunt, imposing themselves on the poor girls until Bob could stand it no more.

He threw back his Jack and water (easy on the water) and asked Toulouse to send a round over as he nonchalantly crossed the room. Tommy was sitting right next to her, sputtering inanities into her ear.

Bob was not a tall man, but that only gave him an intense motivation to be the very best, culminating with service in the US Marine Corps and a recent tour in Vietnam. What he lacked in height, he more than made up for in confidence and power. Tommy didn't stand a chance.

He picked up Tommy in his chair and moved him away from her, down to the end of the table. Before the stunned man could even react, Bob slid effortlessly into his place and introduced himself. He saw that her eyes were the perfect shade of green with just a touch of blue. It was all over for him at that moment.

Bob was a complete goner.

From that day to this one, Bob and Joan were inseparable, painting the South Side of Chicago red nearly every single night. This was the first time she'd invited him into her apartment after a date, quickly disappearing into her room to change. He couldn't believe his own good luck, this was shaping up to be the very best night of his young life.

Joan padded down the hall in her bare feet, wearing an over sized shirt and pedal pusher jeans. She'd taken her hair down, it spilled over her shoulders in shiny, dark waves. Bob had never seen this side of her before, marveling that it was possible that she was even more beautiful this way. She stood before him, shyly holding a book, before lowering herself down to the couch and giving him a kiss. As they reluctantly broke away, Joan handed him the book. It was old and weathered, its pages well-worn from years of use.

"I thought we might read this for awhile."

Bob carefully opened the book. He'd never read it before, although he was certainly familiar with it. They sat closely together with the book resting upon their knees. Joan began to read aloud about the many adventures of Christopher Robin, Winnie the Pooh and Eeyore as they all gallivanted around the Hundred Acre Wood.

Joan's voice was musical, filled with childlike excitement as she regaled him with each tale. He lightly tucked a wayward tress of hair behind her ear, closely watching her every expression as she read. Strangely, as the night wore on, Bob became aware that this was perhaps the most romantic experience he'd ever had. Right here, in a room with this enchanting young woman and the capers of a chubby, stuffed bear.

Early morning sunlight streamed through the main window as Bob sat, completely engrossed in the stories until she reached the very last page and read A.A. Milne's poetic final line:

"But wherever they go, and whatever happens on the way, in that enchanted place, on the top of the Forest, a little boy and his Bear will always be playing."

Joan closed the book with a sigh. As she walked him to the door with a final kiss and promise to see him again later that evening, he decided that his first impression was absolutely correct.

Bob was a complete goner.

Originally Published in "Furtive Dalliance," August 2018

A Christmas Rubicon

Bob hated Christmas. It brought to mind memories of when his parents would occasionally fight after a long night of spiked eggnog.

If he never heard Crosby croon on about the color of Christmas again, he would be happy. He'd take a good rendition of the "Marine Corps Hymn" over that tripe any day, having completed his service as one of "Uncle Sam's Misguided Children" a few years back. It was Bob's opinion that no Marine worth his salt would cavort around a tacky plastic tree or sing about chestnuts roasting anywhere.

"Chestnuts roasting on an open fire, Jack Frost nipping at your nose..."

The song came on over the radio, raising Bob's annoyance even higher. Bob was always getting mistaken for the singer of this song. "The Velvet Fog" was a popular young singer named Mel Torme. Bob did notice a resemblance, but he'd have said the famous "Christmas Song" singer looked like him, not the other way around. Bob was a handsome sonofabitch–Torme should consider himself lucky.

As Torme's signature song continued to torment him over the radio, Bob thought again about how ridiculous the holidays were. So of course, he'd done the only thing a Scrooge like himself could possibly do. He married a bona-fide Christmas freak.

Joan saw him pacing, cradling his snifter of Drambuie. She knew that he wasn't crazy about this time of year, but she'd spent so long on the tree, he'd just have to wait. They'd only been married for a week and Christmas was a few days away.

It was almost a year ago, on December 29, 1965, when she first met Bob Cooper at the Chez Si Bon lounge. A handsome young man with a military haircut sauntered over to where she and her roommate were sitting. Tommy, a regular barfly at the Chez, had just muscled his way into the chair next to hers when Bob approached them. Bob picked Tommy up in his chair and physically moved him out of the way, taking his place by her side. A year later and here they were, getting ready to celebrate their first Christmas together. So why did it look like Bob wanted to throw up?

Joan decided to talk to him just as soon as she could get the tree up, it was the last thing she had to do. Then they could sit under the festive lights and have a Christmas toast. She smiled at the thought as the tree fell over for the third time. Sighing, she picked it up and tried again.

He wasn't going to get involved. *Just keep out of it, Cooper, you're just going to make things worse.* He watched her, so earnest and beautiful, wrinkling her brow as she tried to puzzle out how to get the damned thing to stand up. After the fourth time it fell, Bob decided to act.

Grabbing one of their brand new steak knives, he went to work sawing away at the bottom of the trunk to try to get it to fit in the stand. Bob had never been handy, but he thought he'd done a fine job. He jammed the tree into the stand and stepped back to admire his handiwork.

His new bride clapped her hands with delight. She ran over to finally plug it in, having roped five strings of lights around its drooping branches. Bob went to pour himself a celebratory drink when it fell again. A tiny snowflake ornament flew off and landed in his glass, causing his wife to giggle.

He went back to work, hacking away, twice more it tumbled over. It lay on the floor between them, a Christmas Rubicon, daring Bob to cross it.

Bob had one final idea. He wrapped a reel of fishing wire around the top of the tree and tied it to an old hook on the ceiling. He told his beautiful young wife that he loved her more than anything in the world, but if that goddamned tree fell over one more time, it was going out the window.

Joan tried not to laugh, he was working so hard. Perry Como began singing about there being no place like home for the holidays when Bob went to his tackle box for the wire. She knew his patience was running thin, but he had that devilish twinkle in his eye. She couldn't decide if she was rooting for the tree or to see if her husband would actually follow through on his threat.

In a final defiant act, the wire snapped and the tree toppled over in a great whoosh. Bob downed the remnants of his drink, scooped it up and made his way over to the back sliding glass door. *Much in the same way he moved Tommy aside on the night we met*, Joan thought as she pulled the door open for him. Any anger or sadness either of them had over the tree was forgotten in the excitement of what he was about to do.

He pitched it hard over the third-floor balcony, both of them laughing hysterically as the tree landed right-side-up in a large snowbank. It looked perfect, remaining ornaments in place, with gobs of silver tinsel shining in the moonlight. Joan turned and kissed him passionately, certain that if nothing else, being married to Bob Cooper would never, ever be boring.

Bob and Joan sat out on their tiny balcony, bundled up in the cold Chicago night. They each held a glass of champagne while Sinatra's "O Holy Night" drifted out through their open window, raising their glasses in tribute to Joan's wayward tree below. Cecil in apartment 1B dragged out an extension cord and actually plugged it in, the lights reflecting off the snow and lighting up the apartment building's courtyard.

Joan looked lovingly up at him, her eyes shining as a snowflake landed softly on her cheek. Bob decided that Christmas wasn't so bad, after all.

The Rubicon had been crossed.

Originally Published in "Everyday Fiction." December 2017

Cornwallis Surrenders

It was amazing to him that at a time like this, he should feel so completely and utterly alive. Every sensation was heightened almost to the point of lunacy. The buzzing of flies around a pile of manure, the nicker of a random horse and low, menacing voices all ricocheted around the inside of his head like cannon shot.

The rope was rough and scratchy, causing a maddening tickle in the back of his throat. When he tried to clear it, a sound not unlike the bellow of a dying cow emanated from his painfully dry mouth, causing the assembly of wretched onlookers to shiver in anticipation.

These bastards just couldn't wait to see him swing.

He was to be this afternoon's entertainment, sandwiched in between the day's many bouts of drink and games of chance. Not a single one of them was any better or any worse than he was, they were simply more fortunate in the timing of their transgressions.

Of that, he was absolutely certain.

Percival Lancelot Cornwallis had, thus far, failed to live up to his illustrious name. His mother had suffered from the twin delusions of Arthurian and military glory when it came to her only child, perhaps due to the shameful circumstance of his birth. Nothing, but the resplendence of a great name, would help to erase the taint of a lowly circus performer's fatherless son.

He grew up under the big tent in every dusty, windswept stop along the circuit, crisscrossing the rugged roads of the western plains in every conceivable direction. There were many times, under the loving eye of Miranda, that young Percy would bless his existence as he watched her fly gracefully above his head like a gossamer angel.

Miranda was a magical creature. Dancing and twirling in heavenly abandon as he waited below, the whoosh of the trapeze and breathless sighs of the crowd teaching young Percy all he needed to know about human nature; the incredible high of a crowd's admiration interspersed with a haughty disdain for their profession.

Percy learned very early how to play all of it to his advantage—he was a natural. Up until the day he saw his mother's tiny body, broken and laid out upon the dirt like a fallen sparrow. A simple miss of a grasp had sent her careening to the earth, a final swan dive into eternity.

On that day Percy decided he would no longer be a victim of his circumstances. A fat lot of good that had apparently done him, with the noose wound tightly around his neck, but the point remained the same.

Of that, he was absolutely certain.

She hadn't told him she was married. Honestly, the subject had never been broached.

Percy inherited his mother's fine countenance, with eyes the color of emeralds and a thick head of blue-black hair. Not many of the fairer sex could resist his charms, he was seldom without female company.

On this particular occasion, however, he regretfully considered that maybe he should have let this one pass. Not understanding, until way too late, that his latest paramour was the wife of the town's deputy sheriff. He might still have escaped this particular form of frontier justice if the gentleman hadn't caught him red-handed, fleeing her boudoir with a pair of golden ear bobs in his hastily pulled-on trousers.

A man had to eat, after all. As Percy well knew, a life on the road was one of immense freedom, but very little recompense.

Of that, he was absolutely certain.

He teetered precariously on the back of the wagon. The tree they had chosen for his demise was a sturdy old oak, immense and thick. It also held the distinction of being the only one of its kind around for a mile in each direction.

The perfect hanging tree.

The men stood around in groups, a bedraggled, surly assembly if ever he saw one. A short, rotund man in a filthy overcoat stood at the ready in front of an old nag hitched to the wagon, bridle held in anticipation of Percy's ignoble end. The hastily convened jury passed a bottle back and forth between them, taking turns spitting great black gobs into the dirt.

Looking aggrieved, the deputy sheriff glowered at Percy as the leader of the kangaroo court read aloud his sentence.

"To be hanged by the neck until dead!"

As if he wasn't painfully aware of that already. The words hanging heavily in the air, Percy swallowed deeply and gave himself up to fate.

Percy is five years old, giggling with delight as his mother glides through the air, upside down, and lifts him way up into the sky. They are flying together, higher and higher, before she flips off of the bar. Down they go in a joyful tumble, bouncing into the net below and Percy thinks that he is the luckiest boy in the whole wide world to have such a beautiful momma.

She brushes back a stray lock of his hair and kisses his brow. He is going to be just like her someday, the very best trapeze artist west of the Mississippi and he will buy her a pony. She leans over to him, smiles brightly and says...

"Percival Lancelot Cornwallis! Do you have any last words, you vile bastard!"

The deputy sheriff bellowed with impatience. Seeing no reaction from Percy, he ordered the man to lead the nag away. Percy had only precious seconds left.

The excess rope began to tighten as Percy turned his body toward the tree and began to run. His years of training had served him well, for his leg muscles were toned and powerful.

The man who fashioned his bonds had been rather the worse for drink, allowing Percy to easily free his hands from behind his back, grabbing onto the rope directly above the noose to relieve the pressure. He threw himself off of the wagon with abandon, adrenaline pulsating through his body like a second heartbeat. The reprobate holding the other end of the rope jumped back in alarm, dropping it to the ground as Percy launched.

He hit the trunk full on with both feet as the wagon disappeared underneath him, grabbing the nearest branch with both hands. He kicked off of the tree backward, swinging himself around three times and rocketing high into the sky above the crowd. The frayed old rope wildly lassoed through the air before snapping off midway in a most dramatic fashion.

Visions of his mother floated across his mind as Percy came down, somersaulting gracefully through the air as he descended. He could almost hear the adoring crowd cheering him on in the sudden pandemonium that broke out below.

This was to be the biggest performance of his life and bystanders would later swear they saw Percy smiling as he landed backwards onto the back of the deputy's mount, galloping away with the remainder of the rope trailing him in the dust.

Being the consummate performer, truly his mother's son in every regard, Percy gave them all a final, jaunty wave as he disappeared over the horizon and into legend.

She was a delectable creature.

Pink and soft with the scent of wildflowers clinging to her long, auburn hair. Percy stretched out languidly in the downy bed, being careful not to disturb her as she slept.

The scar around his neck was still angry and raw, all the more so once he remembered that he hadn't yet gotten around to inquiring about her marital status. Not that it would matter. It would only hasten the speed of his departure.

He'd traveled many miles since his final spectacular performance. Far enough that he could actually hear the calming sounds of the Pacific Ocean drifting through her open window.

Percy may have been temporarily forced into retirement, but the show, as they say, must go on.

It was fortunate, indeed, that he was a man of many passions. Passions just waiting to be discovered and revisited, such as the lovely example that now slumbered peacefully at his side.

Fortunate, that is, if he could avoid getting caught. It was definitely time to move on.

He'd just managed to retrieve his shirt from the floor when he felt her warm body stir beside him. She reached out, gently raking his back with her long fingernails and Percy knew it was too late.

Just as his distinguished namesake before him had done, Cornwallis had no choice but to surrender. And he knew, without a doubt, that he would be surrendering again. And again.

Of that, he was absolutely certain.

Originally Published in "Literally Stories," June 2018 and "Frontier Tales," November 2018

The Quest

Time was running out. Only mere minutes were left before it would be too late, his fate hanging precariously in the balance. Chuck pressed his foot down on the gas, trying not to speed and risk getting pulled over. There was no time to waste. He had been all over town, racing against the clock as the final dregs of daylight slipped away into a cold winter's night. If he couldn't find it, all would be lost. Chuck dreaded the very thought of it.

He pulled into the lot and leapt from the car, almost losing his footing on the icy blacktop. Scrambling to the door, he yanked hard on the handle, racing past a bewildered employee about to lock up for the night. Thundering down the aisles, he discarded hundreds of items in his all-encompassing, quixotic quest. It just had to be here, there really was no other option.

On the very last shelf, in the very farthest aisle, he stopped. A voice came over the intercom advising him that they would be closing in five minutes; he'd better go about his business quickly. He moved several items aside. Chuck had worked way too hard to give up without exhausting every last possibility.

As the dust settled on the shelf, he searched behind another item in a last ditch effort. He might fail in his endeavor, but he would leave no stone unturned. Pulling it aside, he took a deep breath and reached around behind. In what had to be one of the happiest moments of his life, the object of his quest sat before him. He pulled it off of the shelf, clutching it in sheer triumph. The voice scolded him over the intercom again, they were about to close up, but Chuck didn't mind. He'd done it. Like a victorious general emerging from battle, he strode purposely to the front. It was all worth it now that he held his treasure.

It was going to be the best year ever.

The little girl's large hazel eyes widened as she pulled the last remnants of wrapping paper off of her final gift under the tree. Claire was just fifteen months old that Christmas. Her very best friend in the world was her pink stuffed animal named "Funny Bunny," they were inseparable. Her parents could already see the first signs of wear on the bunny, wanted to get her another, but it had to be exactly the right one. Chuck had run out on Christmas Eve, frantically searching at every toy store in town.

All of the searching instantly paid off as he watched his baby squeal with delight. She pulled out the blue kitty and hugged it fiercely to her chest. He was dubbed "Silly Kitty" and joined the bunny as Claire's constant companion, one under each arm, everywhere she went.

Chuck sighed with nostalgia at the memory as he got ready to drop Claire off at college. The years had flown by so quickly.

His curly, dark-haired little girl was now a young woman. Chuck could hardly believe it.

The very last items she packed up were her onetime friends, Funny Bunny and Silly Kitty. Very old and worn and full of thread and patches, Claire tucked one under each arm in a well practiced motion. He knew she would hide them when she got to the dorm so as not to get teased, but they'd be there anyway. Just knowing they were there would be enough.

As he closed the door to her room and followed Claire down the hallway, Chuck felt tears begin to form in his eyes. His quest had been a success and now it was her turn. He felt good that her old friends would be joining her on this new quest, from childhood to adulthood.

It was going to be the best year ever.

Originally Published in "Halcyon Days," December 2017

Cone of Shame

Buddy just knew he was in trouble. Big, big trouble. His Alpha roused him from his warm bed early, luring him out into the cold with a slice of mouth-watering bacon. Bacon was Buddy's number one, absolute favorite thing in the whole wide world, except for his Alpha, of course. He wolfed down the bacon, not realizing until it was too late that he had been led straight into the contraption.

Usually, he loved the contraption. He would stick his head over the side as far as his Alpha would allow, basking in the glory of the wind blowing through his long, golden hair. Today was different. His Alpha always got that tone in his voice when they were going to the place that shall not be named. The place that reeked of strange smells, fear, and others of his kind in distress. Buddy would be poked, strangers fussing over him and making him eat strange, bitter-tasting things.

This time was the worst. Buddy recently hurt himself, getting caught in a patch of weeds as he was chasing the bushy-tailed creature across the park. The bushy-tail managed to escape, but Buddy was left with a deep cut. His Alpha was clearly worried, giving him extra scraps and propping him up on the couch. Buddy should have known something was up, he was never allowed on that couch! Then, the next day, the trip to that horrid place. Boy, was he ever in trouble.

Now, Buddy could only pray that no one would see him in such an undignified state. He could feel the edges of it securely in place around his neck, its large white walls surrounding him. It gave him a strange tunnel-like vision, rendering him helpless to attack from both sides. In the neighborhood, his peers would shake their heads and whimper whenever they saw one of their kind trapped inside of one. Buddy walked the long path, hanging his head down as low as it would go. He didn't know what he had done to deserve such a punishment, for surely, that is what the Cone meant. They all knew what it was, dreaded the mere mention of its hideous name–The Cone of Shame.

Buddy curled up on the couch, but it was impossible to get comfortable. The Cone inhibited his every movement, limiting his ability to stretch out. Buddy was well and truly miserable.

His Alpha walked into the kitchen, Buddy perking up his head as he began to smell the tantalizing aroma of steak sizzling away. He sat up and got into his most appealing begging stance, straining to see his Alpha through the frustrating barrier.

His Alpha padded over to the couch, carrying the freshly-cooked meat in his mouth. Buddy knew that he must always wait until his Alpha told him to take the treat, must sit completely still until that very moment in order to get his reward. His Alpha gently placed the steak onto the couch next to Buddy, then gave him a single loud bark to signal that Buddy was allowed to eat. Buddy slowly reached out and grasped the steak in his left hand, carefully ripping off a portion with his right one. He dropped it inside of the cone, chewing and groaning in pleasure. His Alpha was pleased, barking at him and nuzzling Buddy with his long, wet nose. Buddy was relieved to see his Alpha's tail wagging and knew that he had been a Very Good Boy. His Alpha jumped up into his lap as Buddy finished the treat, finally managing to lay down with the Cone in a way that was bearable. He could feel his Alpha checking his wound, re-wrapping the new bandage with his snout as Buddy settled in for sleep.

It would be OK, his Alpha knew what was best. Maybe tomorrow the Cone of Shame would come off and maybe, just maybe, there would be bacon. With that pleasant thought floating through his mind, Buddy drifted off into sleep. He dreamed of bushy-tailed creatures, running as fast as his two legs would take him as his Alpha lovingly licked his hand.

Max curled up in his chair, reaching over to lap up a taste of his finest single malt scotch. This had been a long day and the week was only halfway over. What else could possibly go wrong? He knew that his eldest pup had done something to the vehicle, the left side passenger ski was wobbly, totally pulled out of alignment. His boss was being a real bitch at work, making him fetch her presentations and always taking credit for his ideas. Then to top it all off, the human went and hurt his arm again, setting Max back a hefty 200 bones at the vet's office and causing him to miss an entire day of work.

Buddy began twitching in his sleep as Max went over to nuzzle his long, silky hair. How nice it must be to be a human, he mused, without a single care in the world. Canine-beings in this day and age were so busy, rushing through their days, caught up in the cat race of life.

Max sighed and checked on Buddy one last time before turning in. He was sprawled out on the couch snoring loudly. Even though Max knew his wife would be furious that the human was on the couch again, he left him there anyway, feeling sorry that the poor guy would be forced to suffer another day wearing the Cone of Shame. Hopefully, the wound would heal enough that Max could trust him not to fuss at it, but until then, the Cone must stay.

Max gave Buddy one final lick goodnight. He was human-tired and he had a big day at the kennel tomorrow. After all, he thought as he turned around three times before settling in next to his sleeping wife, a dog's work is never done.

Originally Published in "Corner Bar Magazine," July 2017

Dirt Man

William "Old Bill" Dickerson III was what was colloquially known as the town drunk.

He didn't exactly have his own cot at the local cop shop, but they did keep a bag full of his possibles stored there on those rare occasions when he meandered into town or just had a hankering to pass the evening with Dave Miller, his favorite deputy sheriff and the closest thing to a best friend Old Bill had ever known.

Bill was a "Dirt Man," the senior caretaker at Fort Benson military cemetery and had been for over thirty years. He was given a wide berth just as long as he promised not to ever take the golf cart out on the grounds when he was in his cups, or leave any bottles laying around near the graves.

Not that he ever would. Old Bill was extremely respectful of his silent charges, toasting them each evening as the sun fell over the yardarm and he lowered Old Glory for the day, folding her into precise, crisp triangles. Bill had been an Army "desk jockey" in his younger years, caught in the limbo of being too young for service in Vietnam and too old for the hostilities in the first Gulf War. He was perfectly content with his lot in life, such as it was, serving the heroic men and women in this hallowed place. Old Bill felt it was his sacred duty.

The over sized garden shed in section 29A served as a makeshift home for Old Bill on the nights when he wasn't keeping Dave company. He could be found there, puttering around his personal rose garden and chasing geese away from the long rows of stark white headstones that ascended out of the dark green grass like sentinels in a storm.

Every Sunday afternoon, at precisely four o'clock, Old Bill would make his way across the grounds to one very special headstone placed under an oak tree. The late afternoon sun lit up the chiseled marble as the old man reverently traced the writing of the names, placing a single, long-stemmed pink rose upon the stone. This was the one time he left his bottle back at the shed, for he knew that Lorna would not approve.

His wife and young son, William Dickerson IV, were surrounded by heroes in this lovely place, killed together some thirty years ago in an auto accident. Sundays at four were the only time Old Bill ever knew any real peace without the bottle and he would linger there, sharing with Lorna and his boy all the secrets of his tired old heart.

He tried to picture Billy as he would be by now, a man fully grown, perhaps with children of his own. The despair of such waste always sent him back into the blackness that only the whiskey could dull. One day he would join his wife and son right here, always marveling at the fact that he was standing upon his own grave. They would flip the stone around and place his name on the front of it, giving Old Bill "top billing" as the army veteran. He would request otherwise, if they would let him. His little family would continue look out from this beautiful spot just as they had done for many years. It would be his final wish.

Placing his hand upon the smooth stone, he bid his family a good night, making sure the rose was perfectly arranged. He'd added the inscription *"My life, my love"* to the stone several years before. It was the ultimate declaration that everything he loved, would ever love, was buried right here, in this quiet patch of earth.

Every Sunday when they were married, Old Bill would bring home a single pale pink rose to his wife as a token of his devotion. His rose bushes were the only living things he took care of now, continuing the tradition for Lorna's sake. Since flowers were the only thing he could do for her now, he would damn well make sure to grow the very best roses he possibly could.

On his way back to the shed, he would stop by his favorite places. Bill loved to tend to the very old graves, wanting to pay his respects to the forgotten ones whose families had long ago disappeared into the mists of time.

Fort Benson had started out as a frontier outpost and soldiers had continued to be buried here for well over one-hundred and fifty years. It was just about filled up, only the elderly spouses or occasional veteran still being interred. Before long, it would reach capacity and once Old Bill shuffled off this mortal coil, Fort Benson would be complete.

Bill made sure to always leave a rose at the grave of Frank Lear, a man who had seen action in France during WW1, dying in the Battle of Belleau Wood at the tender age of eighteen. Four rows over, he would place a stone upon Norman Lowenstein's memorial in remembrance of his service in the Korean Conflict. A local hero named Phillip Rogers lost both his legs and eventually died from his service in Afghanistan. Old Bill always made sure that there was never a weed to be found around that fine young man's marker.

Way back in the oldest parts of Fort Benson, he would remove every last trace of the ever-present hoards of geese from the Buffalo Soldiers of the Civil War and the Spanish American veterans, scrubbing down their ancient stones until they gleamed.

A two year old girl, Marjorie Graves, who died in 1894 always tugged at his heart. Her headstone simply read "*Sleep Baby, Sleep*" and made him think of his Billy, so he tended to her plot with special care.

Vietnam vets slept near soldiers from WW2 and every conflict in between, all here together in peace with Old Bill looking out for them all. It was the best part of his meager existence, giving him the only real purpose he'd known since the loss of his family.

The grave of Vito J. Pizzatola and his wife Maria was usually his final stop before he reached the shed for the evening and poured his first three fingers, throwing the whiskey back in a neat, well practiced motion.

As darkness enveloped Fort Benson, Old Bill fell into a blissful, pain-free state, eventually falling asleep on the ancient, over-sized stuffed chair in the corner. The silence of a thousand graves protected his slumber which was why, on this particular night, he was jolted out of a light doze by the soft tones of an old song, floating over him like an errant breeze.

"Over there, over there! Send the word, send the word over there! That the Yanks are coming, the Yanks are coming..."

Bill fell hard to the packed earth of the shed, banging the side of his face on a rusty old shovel. There had been a few instances over the years when he'd had to shoo morbidly curious individuals away from Fort Benson late at night. Kids usually. Halloween or drunken fraternity rituals, running off as soon as Bill approached.

He sighed and reached for the lantern. Old Bill had gotten one of those new-fangled electric lanterns a while back. The damned thing would short out all the time so Bill switched to his trusty old battered one, remembering he and seven-year-old Billy camping underneath a thick blanket of stars, the glow of the lantern lighting up his eager young face. Eyes of green with just a touch of brown. His mother's eyes. Sighing once more in resignation, Old Bill lit the flame and stepped out into the black night.

It took a minute for his eyes to adjust, but Bill swore he saw something moving down in section 30B. He made his way over, careful to walk as close as he could behind the rows of graves, so as not to step directly on top of where folks were buried. Bill had become an expert in this art over many years, remembering his mother's admonition that it was disrespectful to do it any other way.

"*So prepare, say a prayer! Send the word, send the word to beware...*"

The music wafted over the graves, a tinny old-fashioned sound. Like something you would hear in a vintage black and white movie. Old Bill hunkered down as a light mist sprung up from the earth, giving the cemetery an ethereal, greenish glow. He saw a shadow, pacing back and forth, the red tip of a cigarette piercing the darkness.

"*We'll be over, we're coming over! And we won't come back til it's over over there!*"

The music faded away and Bill heard a voice, impossibly loud amongst the complete stillness of the graves.

"Dearest Mama, thank you for the socks. I can't tell you how good it felt to have them in the trench, all the boys were jealous of my warm feet. Please give Corinne my love and devotion, it won't be long now before I shall behold her lovely face again!"

Old Bill jumped back, the young man's urgent voice causing goose flesh to break out all over his body. The man paced back and forth, smoking and talking out loud to himself as if dictating a letter. Bill decided to confront him, there was no earthly reason for anyone to be here at this ungodly hour. He sprung up and addressed the man, trying to make himself sound louder and braver than he actually felt.

"You there! You're trespassing! The cemetery closes at sundown, it's posted right there on the gate. If you do not leave, I will call the police!"

"Please, Mama, if something should happen to me, commend me to father. I always tried to be a man, the kind of man he wanted me to be. Keep me in your heart, Mama. I am and always will remain, your loving son, Frankie."

"Sir! I warn you," Bill sputtered, the hairs on the back of his neck standing at full attention. "You need to leave. Now!"

The man paused mid-stride, regarding Old Bill with large, dark eyes. Eyes that were sunken and steeped in anguish. Bill could see him fully now, recognizing the green khaki of his uniform bellowing out of his dirty, fabric-wrapped boots. Bill was enough of a history buff to know that the strips of cloth that wound around his legs, from ankle to knee, were called "puttees" and completed the "Pershing trench boots" worn by soldiers during the Great War. The first World War, over one-hundred years ago.

The song started up again as the man regarded Old Bill with a sad half-smile, picking up his relentless vigil right where he'd left off.

"John-nie get your gun, get your gun, get your gun! Take it on the run, on the run, on the run!"

Bill backed into a headstone and went tumbling over, hard onto his back. He closed his eyes for ten full seconds, trying to clear his head. Something was very, very wrong. A girlish giggle tickled his left ear, Bill sensing movement as two tiny, satin-covered feet came into his lopsided view.

She was a vision in her lacy white dress, a tiny doll-like creature clutching a faded stuffed lamb in one chubby fist. Bill swiveled his aching neck as high as it would go, straining to see her from his undignified position. Fine, white-blonde curls framed her face, causing his heart to skip a beat as she bent down to him, clapping her hands in delight. She leaned in to give him a kiss, miniature butterfly wings dancing across his cheek, as an uninvited tear escaped from his eye.

"Thank you, Marjorie, my sweet," he whispered in wonderment, her wobbly footsteps running off into the darkness. Painfully he hoisted himself onto his side and grabbed the nearest stone for leverage, lifting himself off of the ground and into another world, altogether.

A symphony of sights and sounds came at him from every direction and frequency, an entire population miraculously appearing as if from thin air. Murmured conversations, disjointed music, laughter. Crying and despair. A precise marching cadence caught his attention, a shadowy platoon wearing Union blue marching in perfect synchronicity right past Bill's astonished gaze.

"Reginald? Are you here, Reggie? Reginald Baker?"

Bill spun around at an old woman's plaintive cry, watching as she methodically searched every row looking for what, he assumed, was her still living husband. A man sat atop Norman Lowenstein's grave, lovingly cleaning his rifle. He sat right in the spot where Bill had placed the stone hours earlier, eventually looking up and giving him a half-salute in acknowledgment.

Deciding that the whiskey had gotten the better of him this evening, Old Bill turned back for the shed. A baby-faced Marine in a wheelchair cut him off, twirling in circles up on two wheels as he whooped and hollered in pure excitement.

"Good to see you, Phillip! Godspeed!" Bill called out as the young man raced away to his grave, the tracks of his wheels leaving ghostly imprints on Bill's perfectly manicured lawn.

The strains of an old Glenn Miller tune reached his tired ears as Old Bill rounded the final bend back to the shed and merciful sleep.

He saw them then. The haunting strains of "Moonlight Serenade" surrounding the couple like a gossamer mist as they danced, swaying together in perfect harmony, matching each other move for move. She looked up into his face, radiant and filled with love as the music played on.

Vito and Maria had eyes only for each other as they flickered back and forth, appearing in the first blush of youth before transforming into a gentle old age, dancing together all the while. Old Bill was happy they were reunited, knowing Maria had just been interred last week. Bill had dug the hole himself. *What a reunion they are having!* Bill thought he'd never seen such adoration in a woman's eyes until a sudden revelation hit him like a freight train, making his tired old knees actually buckle.

Throwing off the shackles of exhaustion, Bill ran past the otherworldly couple and straight to his roses. Even in his great excitement, he painstakingly extracted the perfect one, the rose he had been cultivating for a very special occasion, for he was certain there would be nothing more special than the reunion he would have this night.

As he gently cradled the rose, Old Bill stopped to consider for a moment the possibility that he was dead and decided it was a welcome thought. He quickly tamed his unruly gray hair with shaking fingers and whisked the dirt off of his shirt, holding the pale pink beauty out in front of him like a talisman. Lorna was a lady, after all, and you never went to call on a lady without the perfect flower.

With an energy he hadn't felt in many, many years, Old Bill set off into a joyous run. Past the tableau of a thousand lives and a thousand deaths, the citizens of Fort Benson cheering him on in their shared midnight escapade.

It was the boy he saw first, a gangling youth just past his tenth birthday, staring up at the stars in the sky looking for constellations. Bill tried calling out to him, found himself hoarse with emotion until the words finally broke free.

"Billy! I'm here, son, I'm here!"

His son brought his gaze down from the heavens, locking eyes with his father as Lorna stepped out in front of Billy, stopping Old Bill dead in his tracks. They stood a room's length apart, Bill suddenly becoming nervous to see her again, like a bashful schoolboy.

The cacophony of the dead was all around them, the sounds rising into an ear-splitting volume as Bill crossed the final distance to his love, shyly offering her the rose. Lorna gave him a radiant smile, lifting the dark weight of dread off of his soul as the noise came to a complete stop. The residents of Fort Benson all watched in respectful silence as Old Bill reached out to finally embrace his wife and son.

The Dirt Man had come home at last.

Sheriff David Miller quickly scanned the area before furtively pouring the whiskey from his flask into a shot glass, holding it out in tribute to the grave before him. They'd found Old Bill dead, laid out on his wife and son's grave, clutching a single pink rose. Dave held back tears, knowing how much the old man would have wanted it that way.

Bill had been almost ninety-five years old when he finally expired, a fixture at Fort Benson Cemetery for sixty years. Dave had been his friend, through thick and thin, no matter what the people in town had to say about it.

For years Bill would sit with Dave at the precinct in those lost, dark hours, keeping him sane until that last time over twenty years ago when he suddenly stopped coming. He would never tell Dave what had happened to him, but he seemed completely at peace, like a man transformed.

Whenever Dave would visit him at Fort Benson, he found Old Bill in a frenzy, tending to his garden and regaling him with stories of the different folks buried there. It was surreal, almost like he knew each one of them. Dave knew he never quit drinking whiskey altogether, but he was pretty sure Old Bill had cut back quite a bit, something about wanting to please his wife when he saw her at night. Dave didn't want to remind him that his wife was gone, so he simply listened as the man wove his whimsical tales.

Bill had changed in some fundamental way, of that Dave was certain. For the rest of his long life, Old Bill had a twinkle in his eye, a newfound zest for life. It was a confidence that manifested itself into the most amazing rose bushes Dave had ever seen. When Dave won his election for sheriff, Old Bill brought him three dozen yellow roses and a pint of Maker's Mark. It was from this bottle, that Dave now made his final toast.

He poured one onto the grave before refilling it and throwing one back for himself. Before he turned to leave, Sheriff David Miller placed three long-stemmed pink roses on top of the new headstone, tracing each name with reverence. Fort Benson wanted to switch out Bill's name on the front of the stone with his family's names on the back, but Dave wouldn't hear of it. There were certain benefits to becoming sheriff, and this was definitely one of them.

Dave made sure that all three names were etched on the front of the stone just as his friend wanted, right beneath the inscription *"My life, my love."* The city even erected a small monument in tribute to the "Dirt Man" of Fort Benson, a real badge of honor, placing it at the front gate for all visitors to see.

As he returned the flask to his vest and turned back to his squad car, Dave swore he could hear a faint song in the air, a song he was sure he'd heard somewhere, sometime before.

"Over there, over there, send the word, send the word over there...."

A peaceful feeling settled over Dave as he turned to take a final look at Old Bill's grave, the glorious autumn leaves of the oak tree gently raining down upon his friend as the song gradually faded away, returning Fort Benson back into a blissful, eternal silence.

Originally Published in "As You Were, Military Review," November 2018

The Intruder

The house was dark, the only light being the moon that shined brightly down on an immaculate carpet of snow. The family was safely abed, locked in for the long night, the children fitfully dreaming. Even the family pets were at peace. In a rare moment of solidarity, dogs, cats and the occasional mouse were all resting as one in their peaceful slumber.

Into this perfect winter's night stepped a man, large and intimidating. He circled the house looking for a way to gain entry. The assorted human and animal inhabitants slept on, blissfully unaware of the man's intentions as the clock struck twelve.

The man creeped around the house, circling it twice, peeking through the windows at the darkened rooms within. He was dressed warmly for the weather, the fur of his coat helping to cut the winter chill as he continued to case the house, a bag thrown over his shoulder. He tried the front window, but it was locked up tight, the soft glow of the holiday lights illuminating his eager face. He made his way around to the back of the house, only to find the basement windows encased in bars, there would be no entry there.

The man became frustrated as he checked each window and door, finding every possible way to get inside barred to him. He inspected the garage door, wondering if he could find a way to get in without alerting the family. Could he pry it open somehow? He heard a sudden movement down the street and leapt into the nearest bush, his heart hammering away in his chest.

There has to be a way to get inside, I must be losing my touch.

The car passed by leaving him in blessed darkness once again as he carefully climbed out of his hiding spot, resolute in his mission. There was one place that he hadn't tried yet, it was risky but it just might work. He'd been an experienced climber in his younger years, maybe he could do it again?

He hopped over the backyard fence and onto the deck. A cloud slid by, the winter moon revealing a blanket of bright stars, momentarily distracting him from his goal. It temporarily lit up the sky, revealing the wide, snow covered roof above. He gauged the distance to the roof. He couldn't see it from this angle, but he knew it was there. Thinking that he had run out of all other options, the man decided to try the chimney.

He began by stacking a patio chair on top of the giant aluminum trash can sitting up against the back of the house. Carefully he tested his weight, making sure he wouldn't topple off before he could scale his way up to the first window ledge. He heard an animal sound, almost like a snort and froze in sudden fear, his body pressed up against the cream-colored siding. Waiting for a full minute before resuming his climb, the frigid night air made his nose and ears painfully numb. He latched onto the decorative lattice halfway up the side of the house. It caused the dried-out vines to crackle and break away, his heavy boots hitting each rung of the makeshift ladder.

Slowly he managed to climb up, one step at a time while using the storm drain running alongside of the lattice as a handrail. Being a good sized fellow, every step felt like it would send him crashing to the ground, but still he ascended.

Anyone seeing him in such a state would surely have laughed, his undignified assault upon the quiet home would be amusing if it wasn't so perilous. As if on cue, a light sprinkling of snow began to fall upon his face as he looked up and saw the end in sight. The roof was there, just a few steps away.

The man began to imagine what would happen, how he would handle things when he finally got inside. He started to feel fatigued, forcing his feet to scale the last few steps as his hands latched on to the top of the storm drain. Hoisting himself onto the roof in a final burst of determined strength,he flopped onto his back, breathing heavily while laying in an inch of cold, fresh snow. All he needed to do now was get to the chimney and lower himself inside. The house was older, there was a good chance that the chimney would be wide enough to accommodate him. He flipped over onto all fours, beginning the final crawl to his destination when a sudden movement stopped him cold.

A large black boot came directly into his line of sight, first one and then the other, barring his final path to the chimney. He froze in place and slowly looked up, thinking that he must have lost his mind, this simply couldn't be happening. A huge man dressed all in red towered over him, his bemused expression partially hidden by a full, snowy-white beard. A look to the man's left revealed an animal, bigger than any he had ever seen before, with a majestic head of antlers and a shiny, glowing red nose. He swallowed hard, the fear and disbelief waging a war inside of his mind as the big red man leaned down and placed a hand on his shoulder.

"You've been a very naughty boy this evening, Charlie. Almost as bad as the year you threw the ball inside of the house at your sisters and broke your mother's good china cabinet," the big man said, laughter coloring his voice. "Just because you are all grown up and in college doesn't mean that I can't still see you."

Charlie was too astonished to notice that he was beginning to slide backwards down the roof. He picked up speed and went halfway over the edge, precariously clinging to the greatly-distressed storm drain. The big man effortlessly made his way over to him as Charlie hung on for dear life.

"Merry Christmas, Charlie," he chuckled, his eyes bright with amusement, "and the next time you come home to visit and stay out all night with your friends, please do remember to bring a key."

Charlie lost his grip and fell backwards into the night. In an instant, the enormous reindeer leapt off of the roof and caught him mid-air, depositing him gently onto a snowbank in the backyard. He watched in amazement as the noble creature gently nuzzled him before shooting straight up into the air and rejoining the man on the roof.

The big man threw a giant red sack onto his glittering, golden sleigh. He laughed loudly as he climbed in and gave a shrill whistle, his team of reindeer springing into action with his red-nosed reindeer in the lead. Charlie saw them silhouetted against the glow of the winter moon, the man raising his arm in a final wave before disappearing into thin air.

As he stood up and brushed himself off, Charlie saw that the back door had been propped open, just enough to let him in. He picked up his backpack and made his way to the door. He'd lost his key months ago and kept forgetting to ask his parents for a new one. The warmth of his childhood home enveloped him as he tiptoed up to his room as quietly as possible and instantly fell asleep.

Charlie woke up to the sounds of his twin eight-year old sisters pounding on his door, up at first light to see if Santa had come on Christmas morning. He slowly swung his legs over the side of the bed, cradling his head in his hands and tried to make sense of his crazy dream. The door had been left open the whole time, he must have dreamt the rest. It was the only explanation that made any sense. The smells of freshly-brewed coffee and bacon frying compelled him the rest of the way out of the bed. He'd always had a very healthy appetite.

A quick look outside revealed very little of what had happened the night before. The vines on the lattice were pretty demolished, but the snow covered up any traces of his incredibly foolish attempt on the roof. He must have landed into the snowbank, breaking his fall–he was very lucky he didn't break anything, or worse. His parents would be furious with him if they knew, but so far no one had said a word.

No, the big man was a figment of an overactive imagination, nothing more.

His sisters were squealing with delight, jumping around the cornucopia of gifts that surrounded their Christmas tree. His parents smiled fondly at them as his father handed him a cup of steaming hot coffee, the adults trying to chase the sleep away while the children danced all around them in anticipation.

An hour later, the entire room was covered in ribbons, tinsel and bits of ripped wrapping paper, his sisters curled up together playing with their brand new dolls. Charlie looked over at the tree and saw one last present, small and unassuming, sitting on an outstretched branch. He could hardly believe the "twin tornadoes" missed one, they were a force of nature where Christmas gifts were concerned. He picked it up and saw that it was for him, somehow they had missed it.

He tore away the simple red wrapping paper and found a small velvet pouch, Santa's bag in miniature, trimmed in white. He opened the bag and reached in, pulling out the small object and holding it in his hand. He could feel goosebumps break out all over as he realized just who must have placed it there and why, its message clear and concise.

Charlie held the brand new house key up in front of his face, its golden exterior reflecting the lights on the tree. It was attached to a key chain with a portrait of the big man himself, exactly as Charlie had seen him the night before. His parents looked at him quizzically, each of them wondering if the other had put that gift on the tree the night before.

The intruder sat next to the tree, holding his magical key. He smiled as he relived every detail of his midnight encounter, his face filled with awe and wonder. He was a child again, reveling in the excitement of Christmas morning and the absolute certainty that Santa had come and reindeer really do know how to fly.

Originally Published in "Peacock Journal," December 2016 and "Scarlet Leaf Review," December 2017

Weekly Meeting

Sunday sat at the head of the table, his stern countenance gazing out in disapproval at his unruly colleagues gathered around the table. He held a large golden gavel in his hand and banged it down loudly on the solid wooden block, shaking the table with sheer force.

"Order! I call this meeting to order! You will all take your seats!"

The urgency of his command momentarily stopped the bickering that had been going on since they all convened some twenty minutes before. Monday was the first to comply, clutching an enormous mug of coffee from the local Starbucks, looking tired and lethargic as he reluctantly sat down.

"I propose that the work week begins two hours later. There will be so much more productivity, it's a win-win for all," Monday said in a limp, dejected voice. Tuesday and Thursday stopped mid-argument, turning to him with incredulity.

"That's all fine and well for you," Tuesday snapped, "just go ahead and take away some of my glory!"

"Oh sit down and shut up Mr. Insignificant!"

"I will not!"

"Just because nobody gives you a second thought doesn't mean you have to be bitter!"

"Oh yeah? Well, no one ever looks forward to you, Monday. They all hate you!"

Sunday sighed hard, these two had been having the same argument since the beginning of recorded history.

"Gentlemen, please take a seat, it is Wednesday's turn to have the floor," he said in exasperation.

Wednesday smoothed down her sensible work skirt and sat down primly. "Well, my proposal is to remove the awful phrase "hump day" from the lexicon. It is crude and offensive and I just won't stand for it anymore!"

"Oh come on honey," Friday said as he set his frosted beer mug down on the polished boardroom table, causing Sunday to leap up in distress and hand him a coaster. "You need to lighten up. Here have a drink or better yet, two!"

Wednesday sneered at him, noting with distaste his godawful Hawaiian shirt and ripped jeans ensemble.

"Every day is so casual for you, Friday," she said through clenched teeth. "Some of us actually have loftier goals than two-for-one night at the local Hooters!"

"Two-for-one? Count me in—yeah!"

Sunday banged down the gavel again, trying desperately to recover his patience. At this rate, they would be here all day.

"Do try to control yourselves! Now, does anyone have any more business to discuss before we adjourn?"

Thursday sheepishly lifted his arm, cringing under Sunday's icy glare. "Well, um...I would like to lodge a formal complaint against Friday."

They all turned to look at Friday who was comfortably reclined in his chair, both feet resting on the expensive, cherry oak table. Wednesday rolled her eyes at the sight of his beat up old flip-flops, turning away in disgust.

"Whaddup, Bro?" Friday laughed, lifting his mug in a toast, "feeling a little anxious for the weekend to start?"

"Sunday," Thursday whined, nasally and miserable, "can you please make him stop calling me 'Friday's Eve?' It's so rude, he's just a big bully!"

"Am not!"

"Are too!"

"Am not Friday's EVE!"

"Are t—"

"ENOUGH!" Sunday yelled, his booming voice reverberating throughout the room. "We will have no more of this foolishness! Now if there is nothing else….wait! Has anyone seen Saturday?"

At that very moment Saturday sauntered in through the conference room doors, her exotic perfume trailing behind her. She was perfectly made up, not a hair out of place and they all looked at her with appreciation. All except for Wednesday that is, who had no time for such frippery.

Saturday slowly eased herself into her chair wearing a stunning little black dress and showing off her brand new Louboutin pumps as she daintily crossed her legs.

"Sorry I'm late everyone," she said in a slow, seductive drawl, "it's date night you know and I had to get ready."

"That's OK gorgeous," Friday said giving her a lecherous wink, "it was well worth the wait!"

"Now that is just the end, the absolute end! Some of us have actual work to do!" Wednesday cried, loud enough to awaken Monday who had fallen asleep and was snoring loudly. He went over hard, flipping backward in his chair with an earth-shattering crash.

"I'm alright, I'm alright," he said, jumping up in complete embarrassment, splotches of bright red coloring his cheeks.

"No, you will never be alright because you will always be... Monday–Ha!" Tuesday cackled as Monday tackled him hard around the middle, both of them going down in an obnoxious, fighting heap.

Sunday rose from the head of the table, standing up to his full, imposing height. Filled with righteous indignation, he placed his hands out in front of him as if clutching an invisible pulpit. His voice, rich and sonorous, the music of one-hundred soaring sermons, snapped them instantly back to attention.

"Brothers and Sisters, let us have peace! You are all a vital, integral part of the week! Where, I ask, would the world be without each and every one of you?"

They all looked around, shamefaced as he addressed them, well, all of them except for Friday who cracked open a fresh can of beer, expertly pouring it into his mug without spilling a drop.

"Monday, you are the very epitome of a fresh start, a new beginning with endless possibilities."

Monday got up from the floor, extending his hand to Tuesday who looked at him warily before accepting it, allowing himself to be pulled to his feet.

"Tuesday you are a continuation of this promise, adding shape and purpose to every week."

Tuesday shook his head in acknowledgment, preening in happiness as Sunday continued. "Besides, very important events occur on Tuesdays like national elections and after holiday sales." Tuesday nodded solemnly and shook Monday's hand, both of them taking their seats together.

"Dedication and hard work are what you bring to the table, Wednesday," Sunday nodded to her in admiration. "You are invaluable, absolutely crucial to the success of every week. Without you, nothing productive would ever get done."

Wednesday blushed a little, taking off her glasses and cleaning them as she attempted to regain her composure.

"Thursday, it is on your day that we give thanks and reflect on all the goodness in our lives. Yours is an immensely important day!"

Thursday beamed with the compliment, his face radiant and serene. Friday sat up in anticipation, taking a hearty swig of his beer as Sunday went on.

"Friday, well, let's just say that we all really need you in order to let off a little steam, have some fun after a busy week of labor."

"Right on, Sunday, right on!" Friday said, lifting his beer high into the air in tribute before throwing it back in one long gulp.

"Couples and those looking for love would never make it without you, Saturday. You are a builder of relationships and you're also, well, pretty easy on the eyes, if I do say so myself," Sunday said with a twinge of embarrassment as Saturday gave him her most beguiling smile. "So you see, we all need to work together, we are a team! Let's start acting like it!"

"But Sunday, what about you?" Wednesday asked, "tell us about your qualities."

"Me? Why, I don't like to toot my own horn, but...oh, alright." He said, standing even taller than his already massive height. "I am a day of rest and reflection, a harbinger of peace and faith in a chaotic world, but even more importantly than all of that...I am the day that most football is played!" he said with pride. "With concessions to Monday, Thursday and Saturday during college football season, that is. I don't want to take all of the credit for myself," he nodded sagely to each of them, taking them all in, one by one as he looked around the table.

"Now, let us all go forth and welcome the new week together. I call this meeting adjourned!" He finished by banging the golden gavel one last time upon the block.

"Huzzah!" they all yelled in unison, filing out with laughter and good cheer, the camaraderie between them finally reestablished.

Sunday sat down heavily and cradled his head in his hands. One down he thought in exhaustion and only fifty-one more to go. All of the meetings seemed to go this way and he hadn't even had a chance to prepare his weekly reports for his superiors over at the "Months and Years Department."

Ah well, I'll do all of that tomorrow, he thought with relief as he cracked open one of Friday's pilfered beers. He made his way over to his favorite easy-chair and settled in, putting his feet up and reclining as far back as he could go, his long legs stretched out before him. He had just enough time to catch the Broncos taking on the Chiefs on his big screen plasma TV. The rest of the week would just have to wait.

Originally Published in "Spank the Carp Magazine," September 2017

Aftermath

The ground shook violently, causing Miranda to stagger and sway. She backed up against the wall to steady herself and heard the heartbreaking sound of her late mother's good china shattering onto the floor like ice shards.

She only ever used the good stuff at Thanksgiving, all of her inherited finery with the special crystal goblets. Every year growing up, she'd help her mother polish the silver and china, scrubbing the plates until they sparkled. Each place setting was lovingly arranged, young Miranda folding the napkins so that they would hold the silverware like a fancy pocket. She and her mother always took extra care to make every detail special, reveling in the holiday and each others company.

Pieces of her mother's memory continued to fall en masse onto the hardwood as Miranda fought her way to the door. Frank had taken the kids to the ice-skating rink for the holiday parade while Miranda finished up some last minute gift wrapping. Christmas Day was tomorrow—everything had to be ready. She watched as the tree listed over to one side, sending her children's homemade ornaments flying off in every direction.

Aiden had just learned how to skate without holding onto the side, letting go of his father's hand for the very first time.

Charlotte was already a pro, doing crazy eights all around them, even though at age five, she was a full four years younger than her brother. I need to get out of here, Miranda thought in a panic, I need to find my family.

Miranda stumbled out of the door, falling to her knees several times before clumsily and slowly making her way down to the main square. The town was festooned with holiday cheer—wreaths, lights, and decorations clinging to every lamppost. A loud crack filled the air as snow began to fall from the sky in stinging, white sheets. Miranda desperately searched for any sign of her family, tamping down the hysteria that threatened to overwhelm her with every step.

The storm raged in earnest, snow blowing hard all around her as she spotted them crouched down along the farthest edge of the skating rink. Frank sheltered a child in each arm, every inch the man and protector she'd fallen in love with years ago. Miranda was flooded with relief and terror in equal measure at the sight of them, as another forceful tremor sent her sprawling ignominiously, face-first into the snow.

Just then, Frank saw her, calling out through the howling gale as she regained her footing and dashed headlong across the park as fast as the wind would allow. She threw herself into the circle of her family, all of them clinging to each other for dear life as the lurching, quaking earth finally subsided.

They stood up very slowly, arm and arm, waiting to see what fresh calamity could possibly strike next. When several quiet minutes had passed, they set out. The adults silently agreeing, over their children's heads, that it would be better to ride out the storm at home, as a family.

They both knew aftermath of the storm would be great as they carefully made their way back across the debris filled park. Christmas was still a day away, but Miranda was certain they'd just been given the greatest, most precious gift any of them would ever receive.

The gift of each other.

The little boy could hear his mother's scolding all the way from the back of the store. Sighing, he gave the snow globe one final, hard shake, deliberately trying to get the tiny family inside to break apart. Seeing it was no use, he set the globe back onto the shelf and went off in search of his frazzled mother.

Originally Published in "Everyday Fiction," September 2017

Corpse Flower

The Corpse Flower clutched its hidden treasure tightly, leaves interlocking in a steely grip. The flower would bloom in its own time. It would not be rushed or stopped in this biological imperative, any and all obstacles would be overcome. The evolution of hundreds of thousands of years had brought it this far, there would be no turning back.

This particular flower had not bloomed in over forty-seven years. Forty-seven summers had seen it closed off to the world, forty-seven seasons of a quiet, dormant existence. Life in all its thoughtless cruelty and euphoric joy danced around the Corpse Flower in ten thousand permutations, never once making any kind of impression upon it.

When it did bloom, it would be quite a spectacle, pent-up energy accumulated over a lifetime bursting into macabre fruition. The Corpse Flower would open, gloriously blood-red and rancid, the smell of rotting flesh and death emanating from its core. Seeds from its exultant debut would be quickly absorbed into the atmosphere, tiny imprints destined to grow into their own splendor, carried away like whispered prayers on a current of wind to take root and begin anew.

Upon reaching the end of its cycle, the Corpse Flower would dig deeper, entrenching itself even further and biding its time for another season of blooming. It would go on like this indefinitely, weathering any attack with the sheer, dogged persistence that marked its place in an imperfect world.

If by chance it should die, the Corpse Flower's children would grow and flourish, carrying on its legacy until it became their time to bloom, the cycle beginning all over again. Relentless and resolute, the Corpse Flower would cling to life until there was absolutely no life left.

Only death would separate it from its gruesome task, but then death was its ultimate goal. For only in death would the Corpse Flower finally win the evolutionary battle, killing itself in the process in a blaze of futile, apocalyptic glory.

The Corpse Flower would be triumphant.

To my Family and Friends:

This is a status update I never believed in my wildest dreams I would have to write. It has been quite a battle, but sadly, I have come to the end of the road. The cancer that was in remission is back and has spread. There are no more options for me. As many of you know, I was first diagnosed five years ago and have fought the good fight. My hair is non-existent and I probably could light up like a Christmas tree from all the radiation and chemo, but with great effort, I did go into remission twice. Those days were quite a party, let me tell you (what happens at the remission party stays at the remission party–you know who you are!) However, when I went in for my latest checkup, they found a new tumor. God only knows when or how in the hell this one grew, but it is a big one, the size of a softball. It seems I have used up my lifetime supply of chemotherapy (who knew there was such a thing?) so now there is nothing to do but let nature take its course. The doc says I have a month, maybe more. I might make it to my 48th birthday, but who knows? Thanks to those who have stood by me through all of this, I couldn't have made it this far without you. Stop by and see me anytime, but make it quick! We can share a beer (or two or three or...) and talk about better days. Live every day like it is your last because, well you know. I hope one day cancer dies its own well-deserved death—never give up fellow warriors! Love to you all until we meet again in this life or the next...

Your battle-scarred, but eternally hopeful friend,
Steve

Originally Published in "Literally Stories, October of 2018 and "Down in the Dirt Magazine," February 2019

Battlefield

She watched it fall in waves gracefully down to the floor. She'd always been told that it was her best feature, thick and luxurious with a single streak of white. It was natural, she insisted. A reminder of a busy life with four children. That streak was a trophy, the spoils of battle on a field of teen aged angst where more than once she'd had to pick her hill to die on.

That battlefield had changed over the years. Now she was waging a war upon her own body as the chemo worked its gruesome magic. Her life was a whirlwind of doctor's check-ups, follow-ups and throwing up. Now those very same teenagers were riding into battle alongside her, lances raised and armor ready to fight off the latest onslaught of her disease.

Breast cancer.

A large tumor that had grown in the single year since her last exam. She'd lived the past months in suspended animation, going through the motions as they rallied around her. She worked at an elementary school, the kids all making get-well cards, wishing her well as the first, intensive treatments began.

She watched the white streak finally float by, the remnants of her once prized mane waiting to be swept away. She was Joan of Arc at last, sword held high, her army raised behind her.

She would not die on this hill, not today.

Originally Published in "Cafe Aphra," February 2017

The Dance

How they would dance!

All of their life together was one long, intricate dance, every movement and action perfectly in sync. For as long as she could remember, he had been a part of her world, and she of his.

Perhaps this was why she suffered so, watching his steady decline. There was very little she could do for him now. Only watch and wait for the inevitable.

Lately he seemed to favor his right side, comfort eluding him even in troubled sleep. She spent every spare moment trying to heal him, attempting to meld her body into his as the hours dwindled down to a precious few.

They had experienced much in their life together. Memories of lost children floated through her mind. So much promise tinged with so much regret. How they had survived such calamity gave testament to their union, unbreakable and complete. It would be just the two of them in the end. If she could not make him whole again, at least she would be present. He would not die alone.

He turned his face away from her for the last time, his breathing jagged and slow. She hovered around him, turning and turning in graceful circles as the last vestige of life drained out of his tired old body.

She knew the moment he left her as the water gently unmoored him from his final resting place and carried him to the surface, her frantic movement pushing him higher and higher. She could see, from a great distance, his body being lifted out as she desperately trailed behind and then, he was gone. Gone in an instant, as if he'd never been. Gone away from her forever.

As the water calmed, she resumed her lonely vigil in the place where he had been. All too soon, the mysterious, shimmering surface would call for her, but not today. She began to swim around and around in mournful celebration of her lost love, and how they would dance.

Originally Published in "Ariel Chart," August 2018, "Furtive Dalliance," September 2018, and "Adelaide Literary Award Anthology 2018"

MadDog78

It melded perfectly in his hand.

His fingers caressed the barrel, the familiar weight and heft of it bringing him comfort. Satisfied that it was loaded and ready to fire, Wayne "Mad Dog" Myers unloaded the chamber and carefully replaced the bullets in the beat up old bureau, second drawer on the left. Holding the pistol brought back a wistful remembrance of his Marine Corps days, the only time in his life he'd ever found any real purpose.

Every day he lovingly disassembled and cleaned his sidearm, keeping it well-oiled and at the ready. With a resigned sigh, he placed the pistol back into the drawer and wheeled himself over to the window. Ma would be getting up from her late afternoon nap soon, seeing the gun would only agitate her. Marlene's health was even worse than his, if that was possible.

Long ago, in his boxing days, Wayne was at the very pinnacle of physical excellence. The Corps and his love of a good fight had kept him in top form, corded muscles and washboard abs decorating every part of his massive six-foot-five inch frame. A well oiled killing machine, he'd earned the name "Mad Dog" while pummeling his opponents in the ring. More than one CO had made a hefty profit out of his explosive fists. Now, the only explosive thing about him was his epic meals.

These days, Wayne tipped the scales at a mind-blowing six hundred and fifty-six pounds.

The musical ding of Wayne's computer sent his heart into a nervous flutter. It was Pavlovian, the hold his battered old laptop had over him. He wheeled himself over to a tiny desk in the corner, the only place in the house he felt was truly his own.

PhatChick: RU there??

MadDog78: Hello darlin! I was just thinking about you. Had the dream again, the one where we meet

PhatChick: How did I look???

MadDog78: Scrumptious :)

PhatChick: Betcha say that to all the girls!

"Wayne!"

Mad Dog slammed the laptop shut in a guilty rush, explicit thoughts still dancing through his mind. He may be nearly forty, but Marlene's voice could instantly revert him back to childhood. It was her super power.

"Wayne, sweetie?" her voice was light and lilting, years younger than her actual age. "Did the pizza come yet?"

"Hang on, Ma! I'm coming"

"Judge Judy is about to come on!"

He always brought Marlene her dinner at precisely half-past five. She was mostly bed bound, a state that Wayne's great height and previous years of physical activity had saved him from, thus far. As it was, he got painfully winded walking from room to room so the chair became his legs, Wayne using its metal arms to hoist himself up when the situation required him to stand up and take care of his mother.

Another hundred pounds and he shuddered to think of what their fate would be. Dark visions of her ankle-biter dog,

Peppy, subsiding on their dead, bloated bodies danced through his mind. Mad Dog knew he needed to get things in order before it was too late. Marlene deserved better, even if Wayne thought he did not.

"Wayne? Hurry! Judy's on!"

"Just a sec, Ma!"

Mad Dog furtively pulled open the laptop. He knew he was acting like a simpering schoolboy, but he couldn't help it. Wayne was madly in love.

PhatChick: Did I scare you off??

MadDog78: Sorry, babe. Ma wants her dinner.

PhatChick: Who's on Judge Judy today?

MadDog78: TTFN, beautiful. Tell you more about my dream later....

PhatChick: counting on it...

A single yip informed him that his wheelchair had caught Peppy's tail again. The damned dog was half blind with only one good ear. Not an ideal situation when Wayne had to maneuver his chair around the small house without being able to see over his ponderous stomach. It was a miracle that the Yorkie-poo was still walking the earth, Peppy had to be well over eighteen years old at this point. What a house! Full of invalids, both human and canine, he thought in dark amusement.

Mad Dog balanced the tray precariously on his lap, taking a moment to adjust the pale pink rose. His rose bushes were one of the few things he still took pride in. Wayne loved to see his mother's face light up each spring evening when he would include a rose with her evening meal.

Marlene ate like a bird, the polar opposite of her son. Only a single slice of pizza with nothing but green olives and one lonely chicken wing adorned her plate. Her son was flummoxed at such abstinence. Without eating, Wayne didn't know how he would make it through the long days of his existence. Food was his greatest blessing and biggest curse.

He couldn't remember a time when he didn't think about eating–all day, every day. Maybe his early years in the Corps when he didn't have the luxury of leisurely thought, pounding the ground for miles on end with a pissed off DI yelling in his ear. Even in those heady days, he could really pack it in. Food had become his best friend even in the bleakest of times. It never judged, betrayed or scorned him. It was solace, it was sustenance. It was life.

Only now, miracle of miracles, he finally had something else to occupy his thoughts. The cyber love of his life, Drea Carmichael aka *PhatChick*. They'd met on a weight loss support website, one of the many, many times Wayne had tried and failed to get his health back on track. He knew Drea had lost a bunch of weight over the months they'd been talking, Wayne was her biggest cheerleader. Drea knew he was overweight, but he didn't dare tell her how much.

Whenever she asked him for a picture, he'd send one at least five years old or make excuses about why he couldn't take a new one. He knew he was being dishonest, but didn't want to scare away the only woman he'd ever loved. *MadDog78* was his link to a possible future, or any kind of happiness and he wasn't about to screw it up with reality.

Wayne wheeled over to Marlene's ancient blue Formica kitchen table, Peppy futilely nipping at his bloated ankles along the way. He dropped a piece of pizza crust onto the floor, sending the annoying little Yorkie scampering away in triumph. For the next thirty minutes, Wayne would find peace in his dinner with only the distant strains of Judge Judy to mar his contentment.

The smell of the extra-large pepperoni literally made his mouth water as he eagerly tucked into his meal. A dozen honey glazed chicken wings and a two-liter bottle of soda joined the pizza in Wayne's massive stomach, topped off with an enormous double fudge brownie for dessert. The warm glow of satisfaction quickly cooled, guilt replacing happiness as he took stock of the empty box, pile of tiny bones and gristle.

Mad Dog knew this meal and countless others just like it were killing him, one bite at a time, but he felt powerless to stop. A fresh wave of self loathing washed over him as he boxed up Marlene's leftovers, knowing the remaining seven slices of pizza would sustain her for the next week. She wouldn't miss it if there were six slices instead.

With one last pilfered pizza slice in hand, Wayne turned back to his laptop, the ding of a message wiping away his dark mood, at least for the moment.

PhatChick: so I was thinking, we need to make your dream a reality MD

MadDog78: whatcha thinking gorgeous?

PhatChick: we need to meet, hon. It's been over 6 months. We could at least FaceTime? I want to hear your voice, see your face. You always say we'll meet someday, how bout now??

PhatChick: Wayne?

PhatChick: ????

MadDog78: I'm sorry babe. My laptop camera is broken or I'd

PhatChick: yes, and your cell phone. I've heard it all a million times before. Wayne, you know I have feelings for you. What's wrong? Why are you hiding from me?

PhatChick: radio silence once again. Ping me back when you're finally ready to be honest.

MadDog78: Drea?

MadDog78: Goodnight, honey :(

Wayne tossed and turned, the remnants of his dinner doing somersaults in his stomach. A sharp wave of heartburn caused him to sit up in agony, wishing for death. His mother's constant snoring could be heard through the paper thin walls separating their rooms, although Marlene was very insistent that ladies never snored. The clock on the nightstand told him it was almost three-thirty in the morning as he tossed around his dilemma over and over, searching for some kind of a solution.

He couldn't hold her off any longer, their relationship had progressed too far for that. Too many nights of long, deep conversations and flirtation. She knew him better than anyone else, except Marlene. All of his dreams and regrets, his history and plans for the future he poured out to Drea, and she'd responded in kind. Wayne shared the secrets of his heart, stopping just short of the one thing he knew could drive her away. The reality of Wayne himself.

With a heavy sigh, he maneuvered his massive bulk onto his right side, clutching a pillow for support. He had an important decision to make in the morning. If he told Drea the unvarnished truth, there was a very good chance he would lose her, but if he was not honest, he definitely would. It was an impossible situation, one Wayne did not see himself escaping without getting his heart seriously broken in the process.

"Ma, would you say I'm a good person?"

"Oh, Wayne, of course you are! You are my baby boy."

"No, Ma. I mean do you think anyone, umm..anyone else, would ever like me? As I am... now?

"What have I always told you? True friends will stand by you, warts and all! Martha Jane and I, back in the seventh grade when she…"

"Yeah, Ma I know, you've told me a hundred times but I never had any friends, none to speak of. No one, you know, special…a girl…"

"Hush baby, you just haven't met the right one yet. MJ's daughter is recently divorced, I could give her a call…"

"Never mind, Ma. I need you to do me a favor. I'm going to stand up now. Take my phone…no, hold it like that, wait, no turn it…Ma, no…that's right. Now push the camera button. No, not that button Ma, that one! Okay, are you ready? Now!

MadDog78: Drea, I don't blame you for not responding to me. You're right babe, I haven't been honest with you. I was too afraid. Drea? Are you there?

MadDog78: OK, I know you are upset. Here's the thing, I was so proud when you lost the weight, still am. I wasn't being honest about losing with you, honey. You know I have struggled all of my life, but I didn't tell you the extent of it.

MadDog78: Drea??

MadDog78: OK, so here goes. No more holding back, babe, moment of truth time. I apologize for everything and understand if you never want to talk to me again. Also, forgive the quality of the pic, Ma took it.

MadDog78: One last thing before I send the pic. Just in case this is it.

MadDog78: Drea Marie Carmichael, I love you.

Mad Dog gently polished the pistol with a rag, making sure it was perfectly cleaned, his mind a million miles away. It had been over three days with no response from Drea, complete, terminal silence. He'd tried a few times to get her to reply with no success, his worst fears confirmed. The constant dull ache in his stomach itched away at him. He didn't know if it was heartbreak or hunger, but welcomed them both. Wayne hadn't had a bite to eat in two days.

Reassembling his sidearm, Mad Dog retrieved the bullets from the drawer and loaded them, checking the chamber and cocking it into place. Marlene was taking her nap, he'd left a single pink rose on her pillow and gently kissed her forehead as she slept.

All of his documents were in order. He made sure his life insurance was current and sufficient enough to support his mother for the remainder of her life. She would be bereft, but well taken care of. Wayne prayed she would survive the shock.

Peppy followed along, nipping away at him as he reached the door. Mad Dog threw down a large piece of steak, a final present for the old Yorkie as it ran away with the prize. The steak was half of Peppy's size, it would take him awhile to eat it.

Finding decent clothing at over six-hundred pounds was a challenge, but Wayne did the best he could with his tent like t-shirt and best pair of sweats. He could never fit into his old uniform, but at least he would go out in a semi-dignified fashion. His thoughts turned to Drea, as he wheeled out of the door, down the ramp and onto the front lawn. Even though the outcome had been as he feared, he couldn't bring himself to be angry with her. Their friendship had been an oasis in a sea of pain and he was grateful for it.

He dialed nine-one-one and reported a suicide at his address, wanting to spare Marlene the trauma of discovery. At least outside, there would be less mess to clean up and they could take him away quickly. With any luck, she'd never even have to see his body.

Mad Dog arranged himself as best he could in his chair, pulled the pistol from his lap and placed it in his mouth, closing his eyes on the world for the last time. The slam of a car door jolted him back. His eyes flew open as he quickly lowered the gun and clicked on the safety. Sweat was running down his forehead into his eyes. Wayne hastily wiped it away with shaking hands, his heart hammering in his chest.

A woman was standing on the sidewalk in front of his house, holding a large leopard print suitcase. She had short, curly red hair and kind green eyes. Wearing a nice pair of jeans and tan leather jacket, Wayne knew that she had worked hard to fit into them. This was her "goal outfit," the one she was saving for a very special occasion. They had discussed it many times, he couldn't believe she was actually standing before him wearing it. Maybe he'd already pulled the trigger and she was an angel, coming down to escort him to the pearly gates.

"*MadDog78*, I presume?"

Wayne blinked hard, wanting to be sure she wasn't some kind of apparition.

"*PhatGirl?* Is it really you?"

"In the flesh! I'm sorry I'm late, I've been stuck in airports for two days trying to get here and my laptop crapped out. Besides, I wanted to tell you something in person."

Wayne could hear the sirens in the distance, tried tuning them out as he focused only on her face. Her nose was perfectly turned up at the end with a light smattering of freckles on each cheek.

"What do you want to tell me, Drea?"

"Well I'll tell you, Wayne Myers, if you'll do me a favor and put that damned gun away."

Wayne absentmindedly stuck the pistol into the side pocket of his wheelchair as she came over and took both of his hands into her own.

"I love you too. Now, let's get you up and out of this chair. Every journey begins with a single step."

As the paramedics and fire truck pulled up to the house, Wayne stood up to greet them with Drea at his side helping him to stay upright. He would have to explain this strange situation, but all he could think of in that moment was how he couldn't wait to take her inside and introduce her to Marlene.

Drea would be firm with him. It would mean a drastic change in every single part of his life, but he didn't care. She'd insist upon him going to therapy, especially after today. Marlene would wholeheartedly agree.

Wayne Mad Dog Myers was ready and excited for his new journey to begin, truly alive for the first time in his life. Peppy yipped through the screen door as the paramedics drove off, leaving *MadDog78* to escort *PhatGirl* over the threshold, and into their new shared reality.

Wayne sighed as he slowly lowered the pistol, images of his fantasy meeting with Drea still floating through his head. Marlene would never survive without him, or maybe it was simply a lack of courage that caused him to hesitate. In either case, it did no good to sit in his front lawn with a gun in his mouth, looking like a fool for all the neighbors to see. The old couple across the street were infamous for gossiping, his mother would be mortified.

Placing the gun in his lap, Wayne turned and took a final, longing look at the empty street before wheeling his way up the ramp and back into the house. It was almost five-thirty and Judge Judy was about to come on, he had only minutes to get Marlene her dinner and settle in for the night. Maybe tonight he'd only check his messages thirty times instead of fifty. Hell, it was as good a place to start as any.

Marlene's insistent voice pierced through the window as *MadDog78* wheeled himself through the front door, locking the dead bolt firmly and resolutely behind him.

Originally Published at "Terror House Magazine," February 2019

South Granby Way

On the third day, Gladys began to get worried.

The boy looked just like any average kid that plagued the neighborhood. She and Earl lived here for over thirty-five years. Long enough to be on their third or fourth set of recycled youngish, yuppie-type couples, bringing their fully packed moving vans and enormous hounds to poop in her rose bushes and roving bands of pre-pubescent offspring to roam the street from dawn until dusk, in the long summer days before school mercifully began.

Now, in December, Gladys watched from her bedroom window as they engaged in snowball fights and sledding races. It really was a safety hazard, an awful idea to let them race endlessly down the top of the hill with their dogs chasing behind them, ripping up pristine, snow-covered yards in their wake.

Gladys told them all exactly what she thought about it, on more than one occasion, at the quarterly Homeowners Association meetings, but no one ever listened. Earl warned her it was a fool's errand, they were just kids being kids.

Might as well get mad at the sun for rising, Glady Girl...

Earl was the friendly one. The resident kindly old fart of the neighborhood, handing out candy to the kids every single weekend even though he knew the constant ringing of the doorbell gave her a world-class migraine. They'd never had kids of their own, a fact that Earl lamented but Gladys never had any qualms about.

It was a quiet relief to me, if truth be told.

Gladys' philosophy was that distant neighbors, especially ones with children, made for the best neighbors.

But not Earl. No, Sir-ee, never my Earl. He became their adopted grandfather, the Santa Claus of South Granby Way.

They'd gather around him every Saturday. Grateful mothers in upscale minivans waved to him as their kids convened in Gladys' front yard, helping Earl pile up the leaves, do chores or linger while he regaled them with his latest made-up story. It went on right up until the day that Earl dropped dead of a massive heart attack while shoveling the sidewalk out in front of the Hanley house, two doors down.

From that day til this one, she'd politely accepted their casseroles and bland words of condolence, counting the seconds until they would all go back to their remodeled cookie-cutter homes and leave her in peace. Gladys knew she was no substitute for Earl, never had any inkling to try. She'd firmly locked the door on the kids and their families on the day of Earl's funeral, and that was that.

Now she watched them through her bay window with a battered old pair of Earl's bird-watching binoculars. It was her own way of keeping tabs on the neighborhood from her self-imposed exile, the only real connection Gladys still had to the outside world. Which is how she first noticed the boy, wandering around his house when Gladys knew for a fact that his family had left town for the holidays. She'd seen the cab pull up and whisk them away days ago. There was no doubt about it—that boy was home all alone and Christmas was just two days away.

"Mrs. Crandall, we appreciate the information but when we sent our guy out to check for the second time, there was no one at home, no children, nothing."

"There must be some kind of mistake! I am telling you, I have seen him there for the past three days! At night, all of the lights, including Christmas lights, are turned on and I can see him in there eating at the table. Alone! He can't be more than ten years old, you have to do something!"

"Ma'am, thank you for your concern. We will try to come by once more before Christmas and promise to let you know if we find anything…"

Gladys slammed the phone down as hard as she could onto the receiver. Earl tried his best to get her to use the cell, but the damned thing gave her a headache with its tiny print and confusing buttons. Besides, there was nothing more satisfying than the feel of righteously hanging up on someone. Simply touching a button on a screen didn't cut it. In this, as in so many other things, the younger generations were sorely lacking. That, and keeping track of their own children apparently.

She didn't know the family at all, they'd moved in last spring. Gladys thought she'd seen more than one child at their house, but really wasn't sure. All of the neighborhood kids blended together, one exactly the same as the next.

Wash. Rinse. Repeat. Year after year, decade after decade and so on. It never, ever changes. Except that you knew them all, Earl. Who is this boy?

The boy was cute, Gladys had to give him that. His hair was bright blond and looked almost white when the sunlight caught it at just the right angle through the windowpane. He could have been eight or eleven or any age in between, just beginning to shed the trappings of babyhood. Yesterday, Gladys watched as he danced through the empty house, spinning and laughing, jumping up and down all over the living room furniture. That was when she'd made her second call to the HOA. Gladys wondered for the hundredth time what kind of monstrous parents would leave a young boy all alone for Christmas. It truly was mind boggling.

They should be arrested for neglect!

Maybe her next call in the morning would be to the police station. It was her final, comforting thought before she donned her CPAP mask and drifted off to sleep.

The sudden absence of sound caused Gladys to shoot up in bed. The old CPAP had been giving her fits lately, shutting off without warning. Fragments of her dream conversation with Earl floated across her mind, his voice still deep and calming. His was the only voice she'd ever wanted to hear. It had always, would always be so.

God and all the Saints, how I miss you!

It's Christmas Eve, Glady Girl. Ease up just a little, my love...

Reluctantly, she lifted herself out of the bed, the creaks and pops of relentless age cutting into the silence of the room like a knife. The nightstand clock read half-past-three, a truly awful, godforsaken hour. Since it was quite a production to get out of bed these days, Gladys decided she might as well try to get up and use the bathroom.

The moon was full, lighting her path through the darkened room. Out of habit, Gladys stopped at the window, grabbing Earl's binoculars off of the hook. At first, all was as it should be. A decent dusting of snow had accumulated, giving the street a glittering, immaculate aura. The house across the street was dark as pitch, except for a single candle's glow. Gladys sat in her usual spot at the bay window, transfixed, binoculars pressed up against the glass as she strained to catch any glimpse of movement in the boy's house.

A shadow detached itself from the darkness and moved directly into the front window, the moon serving as a makeshift spotlight. Gladys felt a jolt of shock, gripping the binoculars tightly in her knotted, arthritic fingers. The boy stood looking directly at her through layers of glass. She could see that his eyes were blue with just the faintest touch of gold and that he had a liberal spattering of light brown freckles on his nose. He smiled lopsidedly at her, Gladys easily finding the gap in the front of his mouth where his adult teeth would eventually be.

Her heart skipped a beat as the boy slowly raised his hand in greeting, breaching the long, cold distance between them. Gladys dropped the old binoculars and tentatively waved back at him, quite forgetting herself in the process. She had a sudden melancholy thought, wondering which of the two of them was more alone. In the end, she decided to follow Earl's advice and ease up as the boy slowly retreated back into the dark of his house, returning South Granby Way, and Gladys, back into a peaceful, winter slumber.

Her neck stuck at an impossibly painful angle, Gladys slowly picked herself up off of the bay window seat, the world slowly coming back into focus.

Where in the living hell am I?

A sharp knock at the door caused her to nearly jump out of her skin. Gladys wrapped her old, pink robe over her shoulders and hobbled down the hallway. She couldn't recall the last she'd fallen asleep anywhere other than in her bed. She reached the door, throwing it open with impatience. A little girl with bright blue eyes stood on her doorstep, holding a doll and a large poinsettia plant.

"C'use me, Mrs. Crandall. We just wanted to wish you a Merry Christmas."

Gladys stepped back, tentatively allowing the little girl into her sanctuary. A tall, blond couple followed behind, a large gift basket in their arms.

"Mrs. Crandall, you don't know us but we are your neighbors from across the street on South Granby Way. I am Willa Grayson, this is my husband Pete and our daughter Loretta."

Bleary-eyed, Gladys cautiously opened the door a little more, not used to letting anyone in.

"You may not know it, Mrs. Crandall, but your husband was a great gift to our son before we lost him."

"Lost who? What on earth are you talking about?"

"Our son, Kevin. He died last Christmas of leukemia. Earl was a good friend to him."

Gladys blinked hard, tears threatening to overwhelm her as she tried to process what the lady was saying.

"Dead? Why he can't be! He was just....I just...it's not possible..."

"The Homeowners Association contacted us last night. We were visiting family for the holidays, just got back early this morning. Mrs. Crandall, what the HOA told us seems incredible. Would you mind telling us what you saw?"

Gladys could feel Earl softly place a phantom hand on her shoulder. A gesture he had done countless times in their fifty-five years together.

Everything's alright, Glady Girl. Go ahead and let them in. What do you have to lose?

She heard the little girl behind her, skipping around the living room before settling into Earl's chair. Gladys stepped back and finally allowed the couple inside.

"Come in Mr. and Mrs. Grayson. I am pleased to make your acquaintance. Please, tell me about your Kevin."

Gladys eased into the window seat, her stomach filled to bursting. She couldn't remember the last time she'd eaten so well. The Graysons had put out quite a spread for Christmas dinner, insisting that Gladys join them for the holiday. She'd spent the entire evening in their company, roaming the house she knew so well, looking at pictures of Kevin and reminiscing about Earl. Once again, she felt humbled by her husband's gentle presence in her long life, grateful for the chance to talk about him again. Little Loretta jumped into her arms at the end, promising to come over the very next day with her doll for a tea party and Gladys was surprised to find she was looking forward to it. She lingered awhile at the door of their house, none of them wanting to break their new found connection to each other and their departed loved ones.

The snow fell in gentle waves onto the street below, capping off the best Christmas Gladys could remember in years. The Grayson's house was dark, not a light or little boy in sight. With a resigned sigh, Gladys rose from the window seat and went to prepare for bed.

At the end of the street, almost too far to see, an old man holding the hand of a young boy stood illuminated in the fading street lamp, watching Gladys as she turned away from her window. He raised his arm in a final greeting, the little blond boy smiling up at him, as they turned together and slowly walked down South Granby Way, before disappearing into the snowy Christmas night.

Originally Published in "Marigold Review," July 2019

Marigold

Marigold.

Marigold of a crisp autumn morning, sunlight streaming in to light up her fine blond hair. Soft as a feather, translucent downy lashes framing bright blue eyes. Intelligent and knowing, newborn windows into an old soul. Named for the brilliant golden flower, a ray of sunshine in an otherwise colorless world.

Marigold of the butterfly kisses, her mother's spitting image, apple of her father's eye. A beautiful representation of their years together, blessing their fruitful union. Little lady in miniature, dancing through the corridors of his steely heart, the great man humbled before her tiny form.

Marigold of a thousand days. One thousand sunrises and bedtime stories. One thousand smiles and tears and nights of childish dreaming. Days as her father rose up through the ranks, Bulldog on his way to glory. The furies of battle and first world war coming to an end, a brief respite before an even greater evil rose up to take its place.

Marigold of Kensal Green, sleeping under weathered gray stone. Her mother's anguished cries echoing through the years, her father's resolve forged in terrible grief. A child of sunlight resting in the gentle darkness of eternity, beloved footnote shrouded within the Churchill name.

Marigold.

Ghosts of November

The ghosts of November scratch at my window panes
Distended, twisted branches of a tree, pleading for entry
Silence of a grave on a snow covered hill
Adorned with dried up petals of forgotten flowers

The days of carefree abandon have passed along with them
Youth and warmth and fanciful dreaming
Gone seemingly in a moment, the years rushing by
The ghosts of November dance and dance, wisps of smoke
from a flickering candle

I could not save her in November, nor in the winter as the
world shriveled away in the cold
I could do nothing but watch as the ghosts came to claim her
Seated in a chair beside her bed
As they danced and frolicked and carried her away

The ghosts of November scratch at the contours of my heart
Begging entry as the days grow short, but I dare not let them in
Lest I also shrivel away once more into cold despair

A. Elizabeth Herting

As autumn dies by winter's icy grip, the ghosts of November come to collect their due, before carelessly dancing away into eternity

Poems published by "Terror House Magazine," October 2018

The National
(Heavenly) Pastime

Lizzie

Crack!

Lizzie felt it even before her bat made contact. This was the hit she'd been waiting for. The yellow softball flew high into the summer sky, soaring past third base and evading all attempts by the outfielders to rein it in. She took off like a shot rounding first base with the new two-point turn technique her coach drilled into her all season long. Second, third....the left fielder finally scooped it up and chucked it hard, right into the third base-man's well-worn glove. This was it, the moment of truth. All those hours spent working on her stride and here she was.

Lizzie had always been tall-towering over her teammates and really, every other fourteen-year-old year old she knew. This affected her speed and efficiency, now was her big chance to see if it would pay off. She smiled to herself as she exploded off of third down into the home stretch. She could hear her parents cheering wildly *(Go!Go!Go!)* and mentally prepped herself for the supremely satisfying sensation of the perfect slide. Down she went in an explosion of dirt and dust as she heard the ball land firmly into the catcher's mitt *(please, please don't let her tag me!)*

She made a mental click and entered what she called "The Zone," a place in her mind where time stood still. As if in slow motion, she gave herself up completely to the slide. The seconds passed like hours as she felt her foot firmly make contact with home plate. The crowd was instantly silent, everyone holding their collective breath as the ref bent down and the dust cloud settled..... "SAFE!"

An explosion of sound erupted, teammates running at her from every direction. This was the winning run of the game—they'd finally done it! She heard her father's raucous cheering (always the loudest at every game, much to her embarrassment) and her mother jumping up and down, banging on the chain link fence. The families of her teammates were all high-fiving while she watched the crestfallen faces of the opposing team as they lined up for their end of game ritual: "good game, good game, good game." Lizzie had been on both sides of the equation enough times to understand their disappointment. Coach said the way they handled losing was just as important as the wins and as she shook each hand, she really meant it.

Something about the crowd caught her attention and she looked up to the far set of bleachers. A tall, thin man, possibly the tallest person she'd ever seen, was clapping with wild abandon. He was wearing some kind of suit and hat that made her think of the old time movies her mom was always watching. It clashed with the shorts and t-shirts all around him, setting him apart. He stood off on his own, up on the highest level of the rickety old bleachers, making him appear even taller than he already was. Some sort of enormous grinning giant. Just the sight of him made Lizzie smile, but when she turned back to get another look, he was gone, as if into thin air.

Chub

"Sit down!"

Chub smiled fondly at the memory. The smell of fresh grass and cigars wafting through the air, beer and peanuts, ah what he would give for an ice cold beer! He and his brother-in-law Frank tossing 'em back as they'd yell at the opposing team.

"Steee-rike 3-sit down!"

OK, so maybe that wasn't such a great idea, looking back on it. There were too many times when they'd gotten into a scrape or two, even once when the batter tried to jump into the stands to clobber him. *Man was that was fun!*

Baseball was his life, especially his beloved Chicago Cubs. He'd been dead for well over forty-five years, waiting year after year, on and on into eternity until the Cubbies finally decided to win a World Series. In extra innings and a rain storm to boot. Over one-hundred years it took, but the so-called Curse of the Goat was finally vanquished–hallelujah!

Strike. *Damn! She shouldn't of swung at that one,* his attention was suddenly yanked back into the present. Ball. *Ah, that's better Lizzie.* The pitcher wound up once more and got ready to release. He saw that she tossed 'em high and knew that his great-granddaughter never met a low pitch she didn't like. The ball flew way over her head and hit the fence behind the catcher. *OK, focus girl. This pitcher's all over the place.* Shunk! Ball three slammed into the catcher's mitt just outside the strike zone. Lizzie backed out of the box, looking to her coach before taking a practice swing.

Chub flashed back to a sweltering hot day, sweat streaming into his eyes as his long legs straddled the mound. His fingers tingled in sweet anticipation as he twisted the ball over and over in his left hand. He was well in The Zone, shutting out everything but the sight of the target–his catcher's glove. He rocked back, extending his arm in a well loved ritual. He was locked and loaded, firing it off with every bit of energy he had. The ball shot forward, it's seams blazing in a perfect rising fast-ball. It rocketed towards the batter then...

Lizzie smacked the ball, sending it foul straight up into the air and behind the plate.

Whew! That was close, the catcher almost got it that time. A'tta girl you got a piece of it, the next one's yours.

Once again, he was back on the mound, adrenaline coursing through his body. He heard the crack of the bat and watched as the ball headed straight for him. Instinctively he reached up, his glove held high and caught it in one smooth, practiced arc. The batter scowled at him in disbelief then...

The crowd went wild as his great-granddaughter slid into home plate just out of the catcher's reach. He leaped to his feet (well, as much as a ghost can leap) and waved his old Fedora hat high in the air. Filled with elation, he watched as her team surrounded her and wished, once again, that he could be a part of it. Suddenly she looked up and locked eyes with him. *Her eyes are hazel, just like mine!* She gave him a smile and he felt his breath catch in his throat in pure astonishment. *Can she actually see me?* Instantly he took flight, leaving the nearby rustling of a tree branch as the only proof of his swift departure.

Lizzie

She scrunched up her nose in concentration and started the windup for her fastball. It flew low and hit her father squarely in the ankle, causing him to react with a word she pretended not to hear. "Sorry Dad!' he smiled and waved her off, rubbing his ankle frantically.

Disappointment flowed through her, a tired and sad feeling. Lizzie was a doer. One of those busy people that always had a million things going on and tried to do them all well. In addition to all of her activities and getting good grades, she was a solid utility player, playing catcher, outfielder, third and was a crack first baseman. The truth be known, she loved all the positions and happily went wherever she was told. Lizzie couldn't put it into words, but the game was in her blood, part of who she was.

From T-ball at five-years-old to being the only girl on a series of baseball teams, she eventually moved into competitive girls softball and found her true home. Why then, was she having such a slump? She was a back-up pitcher on her team but knew she still needed to prove herself with that one breakout game.

Lizzie sighed and rubbed her sore arm–they'd been out here for well over an hour. She heard her brother's laughter, running through the park with all the reckless abandon of a carefree eight-year old. Dad wanted her to try again, she could sense his impatience. Her older sister looked up from her sketch pad with annoyance.

"C'mon Lizard, it's getting late-let's go!"

Lizzie felt hot tears of frustration forming as Dad started packing up the gear. She felt a sudden warm breeze pass by, drying her tears and gently lifting the back of her hair. A brief moment of comfort washed over her as she scooped up her glove and slowly walked back to the car.

Chub

"Bobby, come on. Let's try it just one more time."

Chub pleaded with his ten year old son, trying in vain to hold his interest. He was crouched down, his considerable length bent in half, holding out his glove with increasing impatience. Bobby tried, failed, then tried again to get the ball anywhere near his father's outstretched glove. He grunted in anger, throwing the glove down and running off before Chub could even stand up. Not that he could catch him, he was not nearly as fast as he used to be.

He saw himself, even younger than Bobby was now, his mother yelling at him to put the glove down and come in for dinner. *"Not yet ma!"* he yelled as the neighborhood kids scattered. Then, there he was at eighteen, fully grown to his freakish 6'5" height, standing in a line of hopefuls trying to make it onto his first minor league team. The all-encompassing joy when he was chosen, followed by a brief, intense jealousy when his older brother made it into the majors right out of the chute.

I had no choice, but to change my name, didn't want to compete with him.

Robert James Kroupa became Robert James Cooper with the stroke of a pen, and he never looked back. *Ah, the glory days!* Hundreds of memories flew at him all at once. His first strikeout followed by the pain of his first walk. The countless wins and losses, highs and lows. The Babe coming to town as a favor to his manager and letting Chub use his bat. *God, how I loved it!* The game was in the very fabric of his being until....

He snapped out of old memories as Lizzie let go of the pitch and hit her father at full speed. His heart dropped as he saw her shoulders fall, felt her disappointment. *She's giving up. She has all that power, now she just needs confidence.* How could he possibly help her? She saw him once, could it happen again?

Chub felt a familiar pang of loss, remembering the day he had to quit the team.

"I'm so sorry coach, Pa lost his job. My family needs me."

He thought of the headlines, "Stock Market Crash!" and recalled the desperation of those long ago days. He saw a beautiful woman, *(Adele)* and fondly recalled his single minded pursuit of her. *God, how I chased that woman to the ends of the earth and back, what a journey that was!*

Her family was straight off the boat from Lithuania and he vaguely remembered getting his nickname from them. "Chub and Gug," they called them, Bob and Adele, some foreign meaning behind the name that he couldn't quite recall. She was a divorcee with a small child at the time, quite scandalous in those days. Chub raised her son as his own and then, Bobby came along. His only natural born child.

His great-grandson ran past him, the very image of Bobby at that age. Chub reached out to him, then pulled back.

I gave it all up but it was always with me, this love of the game. Ah, what might have been?

He remembered the day when Bobby told him he would never play baseball again.

"I'm sorry Dad, it's just not for me."

Chub swallowed back the old bitterness. *How could my own son not love the game? What failing of mine caused this?* Then, he recalled with pride, Bobby joining the Marine Corps, serving bravely in Vietnam. *He came home, a fine man, had a family...*

Lizzie walked by, slumped over and Chub sprung into action. She couldn't see him this time, but she would feel him. He poured his heart out into the summer breeze, sending her all of his love in a single long breath.

Lizzie

Closing her eyes, she desperately tried to summon The Zone. Coach just said she'd be pitching today. Taking a deep breath, she pushed all worry to the back of her mind, willing the dull throb in her arm to go away. She was excited, anxious to get in there and give it a whirl. This was the third and final game of the tournament, with the winner earning the chance to move on to the Championships. She wound up and snapped it.

"Not half bad kid!"

Turning, she saw him there, casually leaning up against a tree. He had a kind face, a warm glow, almost appearing to be back-lit against the tree. Lizzie had a quick flash of recognition, knowing him from somewhere, but where? A snippet of an old show on late night TV ran through her mind, *"to the moon Alice!"* What was that? He looked just like the tall man, the one who played the best friend on that show.

"Art Carney from the Honeymooners", he answered her, "yeah, I get that a lot."

His eyes crinkled in amusement, she saw they were hazel, just like.... *Wait! Did I say that out loud?*

"Now, I'm no softball pitcher, mind, but I can see you've got the fundamentals, Lizzie, now ya gotta put some spit and grit into it."

He plucked the ball from her outstretched hand and threw it dead on into the net.

"Let me give you a couple of general pointers."

Lizzie listened with rapt attention, marveling that he seemed to know her so well. He adjusted her stance a little, showed her his "world famous lock and load technique," all the while regaling her with stories about his past days of glory. Babe Ruth? Seriously? She could hardly believe it.

Time flew fly by and Lizzie discovered she was sad to leave. He started to walk away then stopped, turning back to her.

"Always remember Lizzie-The Zone is in your heart as well as your head and you, kid, are all heart."

Goosebumps broke out all over her arms, she was completely stunned by his words.

"Wait! You know about The Zone?"

Chub tipped his old hat to her in tribute.

"Know about it? Kid, I invented it." He winked and gave her pitching arm a gentle squeeze as he headed over to his favorite bleachers.

Lizzie felt a sudden warmth spread throughout her arm, all soreness disappearing in an instant. She watched him walk away, the sound of his tuneless whistling filling the air. Lizzie smiled, a slightly puzzled expression on her face before shaking it off. She grabbed her glove and started out for the field.

Chub

She's really holding her own. Lizzie walked a few, but was also putting out a fair amount of strikes. He felt his fingers tingling, turning an imaginary ball round and round in his hand. Out on the field, Lizzie did the exact same motion, matching him in perfect synchronicity. She wound up and he noted with satisfaction that she was picking up the "lock and load" with great speed.

Strike, good! She really needed that one, the first two pitches were balls and this was the last inning. If they could hold 'em here, Lizzie's team would win the game. He was on the edge of his seat, literally floating just above the bleachers. Was he ever this nervous during his own games? Now he understood why Lizzie's mom paced back and forth while her dad crossed his arms anxiously. Ball three. *Damn, that was almost there. C'mon girl, go there, get into The Zone.* Crack! He looked up in time to see the ball cross the white line, clearly a foul. *It's OK-breathe Chub, breathe!* He laughed at the irony, the butt of his own private joke. Chub hadn't had to worry about breathing in a very long time. He sent out all of his energy, trying to reach out to her by sheer force of will. *Here it comes, the last pitch of the game.* Chub hunkered down for what felt like the longest moment of his after-life.

Lizzie

Lizzie saw him out of the corner of her eye, out in the distance. She felt that same warm energy envelop her again. The Zone had never been more welcoming, all traces of self-doubt evaporated in an instant. She felt a tingle in her hand and began to turn the ball in a slow, deliberate motion. They were playing hard today, she had no doubt that not a single pair of pants would come out unscathed in the end, grass and dirt covering every inch. Lizzie had never felt more connected to them, so proud to be a part of this team.

An electric hum surrounding her, adrenaline coursed through her veins as she locked, loaded and fired it off. Crack! The batter hit it hard and took off, kicking up a big cloud of dirt in her wake. Lizzie watched as the ball sailed by her and landed right behind the waiting glove of the second baseman. The runner went full throttle as the second baseman scooped it up and fired it off to first, all of them praying it got there in time. She looked up for a split second, searching for him, found him hovering *(floating? What?)* over the bleachers in an attempt to get a better view then...OUT!

The crowd erupted as the field turned into a hive of frenzied activity. They all rushed together in pure glee, the entire team becoming one. She found her parents in the crowd hugging, jumping up and down with pride. Even her sister and little brother were celebrating–a true miracle, indeed. Her coach slapped her on the back, picking her up in a great bear hug. She turned to find him one last time, wanting to share this moment with him, the greatest moment of her softball life. The top bleacher was empty, just as she suspected it might be, but it really didn't matter.

Lizzie was not sure of a lot of things but she knew one thing with absolute certainty. He would always be there watching over her, her guardian angel, for they were connected by one thing that can never be broken. Love of the game.

Chub

Chub had often heard the phrase "bursting with pride" but until now, he always thought it was just an expression. He literally felt his energy coming apart at the seams as the first baseman caught that ball. He rocketed up into the air in his joy, a burst of pure light, before landing back down on what he fondly thought of as his bleacher.

He looked over at Lizzie's parents, her mother–Bobby's only child—as celestial tears clouded his vision. His family, his and Adele's. It was all worth it and he wouldn't change a damned thing. He watched as Lizzie's coach picked her up and lead her around the field. *She's going to be just fine. My Lizzie.*

He took one last look before taking his leave. After all, he had to come back for the Championships and in the meantime, he had just enough time to make it to his weekly heavenly poker game.

A sudden burst of air quickly subsided as a battered old Fedora gently floated down and landed on the top step of the bleachers.

Originally Published in "Commuter Lit," January 2019

Original Sin

Kristina Milnius had perfect hair.

She sat directly in front of Bobby in Sister Mary Bernard's third-grade class at St. Casimir's Primary School in Oak Lawn, Chicago. Her silky blonde hair flowed down her back, reaching past her waist like a princess in a fairy tale. It was the cause of endless fascination for young Bobby Cooper, bored as he always was, by the nun's endless droning.

On and on Sister Bernard lectured, her colorless voice lulling him into a doze as he focused on Kristina's polished tresses. They were arranged into two amazingly long braids. He couldn't decide if one was just slightly longer than the other or if boredom was causing his mind to drift. Bobby wanted to touch them more than anything else in the world, feel the heft and weight of them.

It wasn't that he particularly liked Kristina Milnius. All girls were strange creatures and better left alone. They didn't like mud pies or stick ball, kick the can or catching frogs down by the creek. They smelled funny and giggled a lot. No, Bobby's interest was purely academic.

He longed to know how her hair looked out of the braids. How long it took her mother to arrange them each morning or what it felt like to have that much hair. Bobby's father shaved him every month or so, "high and tight" he would always say, so Bobby really had no idea what it was like. If he reached out and picked up a braid would Kristina even notice?

Sister Bernard rapped her ruler hard on Bobby's desk causing him to jump. She'd corrected him more than once about daydreaming, his mother gave him a good whack about it just last week. He shot to attention, folding his hands on the desk and nearly knocking over his ink pot. Bobby had gotten in trouble many times for spilling ink and was relieved to see it wobble, then settle back into the upright position. Ink was not cheap and waste was a sin. Bobby rubbed his knuckles in fear, terrified of the nun's swift, punishing ruler.

Satisfied that she'd reclaimed his attention, Sister Bernard passed him by without missing a single word in her lesson. Bobby felt his heart hammering in his chest as the recess bell mercifully rang.

The previous night had been a rough one. Bobby's mother was so mad that she'd yelled at him in Lithuanian, reverting back to the language of the old country. Sister Bernard wouldn't hesitate to phone her again—Bobby needed to be on guard. He sat up ramrod straight in his chair, hands clean and demurely folded as Kristina sat down. She was a vision in powder blue with two tiny matching bows in her golden-white hair.

All self-control abandoned him as a single shimmering braid flopped onto Bobby's desk. A quick glance around the classroom found Sister Bernard facing the blackboard, his classmates all obediently copying away. There would never be a more perfect time.

Bobby reached down to claim his prize. He knew he was committing a grave sin, but felt powerless to resist. Pillowy and soft, he squeezed it lightly between his fingers, making sure not to alert Kristina. Such was the length of her hair that she couldn't feel his intrusion as he picked it up, fascinated by its silken texture. Before he knew what he was doing, Bobby pulled it slowly across the desk and plunged the tip of the braid into his open inkpot.

Mesmerized, Bobby watched the ink move its way up Kristina's braid, an enormous sucking fountain pen. Frantically he looked around, stunned that he seemed to be the only witness to this miraculous event. When the blackness had consumed over half of the hair, Bobby gently pulled it out, taking a quick moment to refill his ink. It seemed a real shame that the other braid should not be included in such an exciting experiment so Bobby decided to try his luck again. He pulled the other braid onto his desk and dipped it in.

The ink moved faster this time, beating its twin as it climbed higher and higher, past Kristina's shoulders before Sister Bernard finally turned around. Bobby kept his eyes on the braid, completely entranced as the nun screamed in alarm. Bobby knew he would be in very, very big trouble, but he also knew in his ten-year old-mind that it was completely worth it.

Bobby Cooper had a hard time sitting for the next few days. Kristina Milnius' mother joined his own in berating him in a fiery mixture of Lithuanian and English, such was the enormity of his transgression. He stood in the corner all the next day followed by three weeks of cleaning erasers. His mother banned him from the radio, there was to be no "Lone Ranger" for two months. Even his father got in on Bobby's punishment, making him rake up all the leaves. He did allow Bobby to burn them, so it wasn't a complete wash.

The hardest part had been apologizing to Kristina herself. He thought her new short hairstyle was quite becoming and told her so, earning a slap on the back of his head for his trouble. His parents knew Kristina's mother and she was still on the warpath. Bobby's mother was not amused, although he did notice a slight twinkle in his father's eye whenever the subject of Bobby's "Original Sin" was mentioned.

From his new seat across the classroom, Bobby looked for Kristina. Sister Bernard seated him behind Joey Zulanis, knowing that Bobby wouldn't touch his hair without getting a knuckle sandwich in return. He saw that Kristina's short hair was pulled back with a pink headband, silky tendrils escaping in curls around her face and Bobby began to think that maybe girls weren't so bad after all. As he settled into daydreaming, he thought that his first impression was still correct.

Kristina Milnius had perfect hair.

Originally Published in "The Fiction Pool," January 2018

About the Author

A. Elizabeth Herting has had short fiction stories featured in many different publications, including podcasts, reprints and poetry. She also has experience with non-fiction and as an online copywriter.

When not writing or driving kids around, she is also a member of Sweet Adelines International, a worldwide women's singing organization. She sings and competes as a Lead in a ladies barbershop quartet called Deja Vu, voted "Audience Choice/Open Division" in their regional competition for 2015, 2016, 2018 and 2019; Skyline Chorus, an International award winning group of 140 singers in Denver, Colorado; and Bella Voce, a regional first-place medaling small chorus based out of Craig, Colorado. She has been singing and performing all over the great state of Colorado (and beyond!) since 2002 and also helps to create shows and scripts as part of a writing team for those wonderful musical groups.

A. Elizabeth was proud to be selected as a Finalist in the "Adelaide Literary Award, 2018 & 2019 Short Story Anthologies and 2019 Poetry Anthology." Her story "Sourdough's Cabin" was chosen as "Readers Choice" in the November 2017 edition of "Frontier Tales" for a future anthology. She has also had stories featured in short story anthologies: "Write to Meow," "Weird Reader 2017 Edition" and "Ghostlight, the Magazine of Terror."

"Postcards From Waupaca" is her second collection of short stories. The first one, "Whistling Past the Veil" was published by "Adelaide Books" in 2019. A. Elizabeth has also completed her first novel called "Wet Birds Don't Fly at Night" that she eventually hopes to find a home for. aeherting.com, twitter.com/AEHerting, facebook.com/AElizabethHerting

www.ingramcontent.com/pod-product-compliance
Lightning Source LLC
Chambersburg PA
CBHW020023030726
47499CB00007B/2242